past

old

MELVIN BURGESS

trust

# AN ANGEL FOR MAY

young

trust

suspicion

safety

danger

past

present

old

young

trust

PUFFIN BOOKS

present

old

*For Mum and Dad*

PUFFIN BOOKS

Published by the Penguin Group
Penguin Books Ltd, 80 Strand, London WC2 0RL, England
Penguin Putnam Inc., 375 Hudson Street, New York, New York 10014, USA
Penguin Books Australia Ltd, 250 Camberwell Road, Camberwell, Victoria, Australia
Penguin Books Canada Ltd, 10 Alcorn Avenue, Toronto, Ontario, Canada M4V 3B2
Penguin Books India (P) Ltd, 11 Community Centre, Panchsheel Park,
New Delhi – 110 017, India
Penguin Books (NZ) Ltd, Cnr Rosedale and Airborne Roads, Albany, Auckland, New Zealand
Penguin Books (South Africa) (Pty) Ltd, 5 Watkins Street, Denver Ext 4,
Johannesburg 2094, South Africa

Penguin Books Ltd, Registered Offices: 80 Strand, London WC2 0RL, England

www.penguin.com

First published by Andersen Press Ltd 1992
Published in Penguin Books 1994
10



Made and printed in England by Clays Ltd, St Ives plc



British Library Cataloguing in Publication Data
A CIP catalogue record for this book is available from the British Library

ISBN 0–140–36981–3

# Chapter 1

A boy ran up the hill. Halfway up he began to cry but he didn't stop. At the ridge just above the hidden valley he paused and turned a tear-stained face back down. He could see his house from here. It stood at the edge of the town and gazed blandly at him over the cricket pitch and the allotments where his dad used to grow vegetables and strawberries. Tam stuck his tongue out at it, made the V-sign, stuck his backside out and made a rude noise, but none of it expressed how he felt. Finally he shouted, 'Bloody old bag!'

A few sheep looked up at him in surprise. One ran off with a lamb. They stopped a few metres further on and stood looking over their shoulders at him to see what he would do next.

'Maa-a!' shouted Tam. The sheep began tearing at the rough grass. Tam felt foolish. He imagined that his mother was standing grimly at the window watching him. Or was she curled up in the armchair in the corner of the sitting room, crying again with her black eyes?

Tam would have preferred to live with his father anytime, although he knew the flat in Bradford wasn't half the place Cawldale was. His dad said it was too small for Tam to come and live with him and Julia but Tam knew the real reason. The flat was full of Julia's children. His dad had another family. He was left behind to cope with his miserable mother.

Tam jumped from the crest of the ridge and ran down towards the ruined farmhouse that crouched in the hidden valley. Low walls and scattered stone were all that remained, but at one end half the chimney stack still stood. You could light a fire and it still worked. The local people knew the ruins by their old name, Thowt It – short for Who'd-a-thowt-it Farm, because who would have thought it, finding a farm hidden away up there, when there seemed to be nothing but that long hill and the sheep . . .

The wind was beginning to whip up hard, icy drops of rain that stung his face. Tam had run out with no coat and he was frozen already but he wasn't going home, not yet, not now – not ever, the way he felt just then. He'd catch cold first and die out here where the coarse grass began to give way to the heather from the moor above. One day someone would find his skull staring down at the town, just as he had once found a sheep's skull, and they'd wonder who he was and how he got there. Tam felt that he could do anything to hurt his mother.

As he dropped down into the secret valley the wind softened. It was still hard enough. A line of Scots pines that had once been a windbreak flickered and bent in it. Now that the sheep roamed freely over the wrecked homestead they ate any young seedlings that sprouted up and the colony of trees was dying out. The line stood against the open moorland above like shattered posts. Some trees were broken off, some were still in their prime. But there were no saplings. The sheep ate everything.

If you had to be miserable the old farm was a good

place to do it. There was no one there to see you except a few untidy sheep and the little brown and grey birds that flicked and chirruped over these low moorland fields.

Tam sat down in a corner of one of the rooms. The noises of the moor – the wind, a curlew calling some way off, a little bird chittering nearby – carried on above his head. It was a strange feeling, sitting in a room with the rain still speckling your skin and the wind in your hair. To one side of him was the tall wall with the chimney in it. People had come for picnics and lit fires there. A circle of stones had been laid out in front of it, and at night, staring at a blaze you could imagine that this was still a home and that behind your back the rooms still stood and people slept and talked and lived. Perhaps they did.

There was a noise beside him. Tam looked across and almost jumped out of his skin because there was a dog sitting next to him. He hadn't heard a thing – not a breath, not a crumple of grass underfoot. The dog looked at him and thumped its tail.

'Good dog,' said Tam cautiously. It seemed like a nice dog, but it was a bit close. It was a sheep dog mongrel, one of those dogs with lots of hair and a fringe that looked intelligent and foolish at the same time.

The dog was delighted and tried to lick his face. Tam squirmed. 'Gerrof!' he exclaimed. But the dog thought it was a game and began huffing and licking and then it growled and tried to pull at his clothes with its teeth, but ever so gently.

Tam was a bit nervous of strange dogs, but this was

a good dog. They had hardly met for a minute and here they were, wrestling on the grass. It was impossible to be cross, the dog was so good natured. Tam had a peek and saw the dog was female.

'What are you doing out here, girl?' asked Tam. He looked around for the owner. There was no one in sight. Probably they were not far off, though.

Now the dog got up and began snuffling around the wall. Rabbits, thought Tam. He wanted the dog to catch one. The dog snuffled and scratched busily away at the turf. She got terribly excited at a hole in the wall and began barking at it. Tam laughed. She was making far too much noise to catch anything. But she was a good dog. She knew enough to leave the sheep alone, and she was so full of bounce.

Now the funny old thing gave up the rabbits, had a pee by the hole in the wall, scratched a few times and came up to Tam to be patted. She sat up on her legs begging and began nodding her head up and down, just as if she were talking. 'Yes, yes, yes, yes . . . ' she seemed to say. Someone must have taught her.

'I haven't got anything for you,' laughed Tam. But the dog just wanted to play.

Tam ran up above the ruin to see if he could spot the owner, but although he got a view right up and down the path he saw no one. Perhaps the dog was a stray. She had run on ahead and now she came rushing back, hair flowing all over her face. She had a stick in her mouth – a small branch, really; it was much too big, she could barely lift it off the ground. Tam broke a bit off. When the dog tried to snatch it, he felt at her neck. There was a worn leather collar; the dog was no stray. It was stupid, anyway. His mother would never let him have a dog.

Tam waggled the stick in the air. The dog barked delightedly, pranced around, whining and yelping. She was off as if she'd been fired out of a gun when Tam finally threw it. Then she came running back and dropped it on his feet for a repeat.

Quite suddenly it began to rain hard. The hills and the town below them and even the ruined buildings nearby turned grey. Tam ran as fast as he could to shelter behind one of the farmhouse walls. By the time he was halfway there he stopped running. There was no way he could get any wetter. It was a downpour. Now he'd get into more trouble, but he didn't care.

The rain seemed to be coming from every direction at once. The only place where he could get out of it was actually under the chimney. It was filthy with mud and wet ashes but Tam crawled deliberately right into them. His school clothes, already sodden and muddy where he had fallen playing with the dog, got black with the ash. It was school again tomorrow; his mother would have to wash them for him overnight.

The wind blew the rain onto him even here. As soon as the dog crept beside him she shook herself violently.

'Hey, you idiot!' Tam shouted. It was horrible – worse than the rain. She looked at him in surprise, wagged her tail and tried to lick his face. Really, it was quite impossible to be cross with her for more than a moment.

The boy and the dog sat in the wet ashes together

and looked out at the rain falling in sheets. They could hear the soft sound of it as it struck the fields and stones outside. The dog had begun to smell with the wet and Tam was soaked through and cold to the bone and filthy. But for all that he felt cosy, snuggled up in the chimney with this friendly dog – as if he were warm and dry at home with a wet blowy day outside and a roaring fire to stare at, instead of these sheets and sheets of rain.

As Tam sat tucked away behind the curtain of rain, something strange began with a smell. He sniffed the air and it took him a moment to recognise it because it was so out of place. Tam smelled toast. He laughed out loud. Everything was sodden and dripping, there wasn't a spark of fire for miles. But there it was, the smell of nice brown toast just come out of the grill and ready for the butter to go on. Suddenly it was so real he was certain someone was near with toast and his mouth began to water. The dog seemed to smell it as well because she began dribbling and wagging her tail. Tam peered out through the layers of rain wondering who could be cooking toast out in that lot. And he saw the girl.

She was sitting directly in front of him. There was a fire between them – in fact Tam was sitting in the fire but he could only feel a soft heat from it. The fire was low, no flames; a bright red glow. Behind the girl was a long room with carpets and rugs on the boards. The room was very bare and strange. A big pendulum clock ticked heavily on the wall. The girl was kneeling in front of him – in front of the fire. She had a long brass fork in her hand with a piece of toast on the end of it. She was making toast by the fire and Tam and the dog were sitting in the fireplace.

The girl was looking directly at him and Tam knew that she could see him too. The dog began nodding her head again – yes, yes, yes. The girl frowned. She said, 'Winnie?' in a strange, flat voice.

The dog wagged her tail. She seemed quite at home. She suddenly leaned forward and tried to take the piece of toast off the end of the fork with her teeth.

'Hey!' cried the girl. Tam could hear her shout as he could feel the soft warmth of the fire – distantly. She jumped back a little and the toast fell off the fork, through the dog's nose and into the fire where it began to burn. Tam laughed out loud; the girl looked at him crossly.

'Go away!' she shouted. 'Bad dog!' she added. The dog whined and lay down. And then the wind blew in on him, right in with a gust of rain and it all vanished as suddenly as it had come. Tam was sitting with a dog in the old fireplace, getting his school trousers filthy with wet charcoal and mud and there was nothing but a vague smell in the air. The dog slobbered and licked her chops. Tam sniffed again, and it was gone.

What had he seen? The vile rain poured down where there had been a snug household. There was a low dip in the wall to his left where a vase of daisies and a photograph on a stand had stood on the window-sill a few seconds ago. Had he seen ghosts – or had he been a ghost himself?

The dog whined and crouched into the mud by his

leg. The girl had known her. Suddenly Tam wanted to go home. He said, 'Winnie?' and she looked up and wagged her tail. She jumped up and began licking his face again.

'Down!' Winnie crouched again. Cautiously Tam thumped her sides and her ribs thudded hollowly. She was a real dog all right.

The rain seemed to have fallen off only slightly; it looked set solid for hours yet, falling violently out of the sky in the wind. Tam peered anxiously out to make sure that all traces of the vision were gone. There was a figure standing in the rain.

Now Tam really was frightened, because that was no human figure. He could not make it out properly in the thick rain, but it stood slouched and crooked, and there seemed to be a horrid lump on its neck. The figure was just standing there not even trying to get out of the downpour. Everything about it was wrong – the shape of the head, the way it stood, everything.

But Winnie gave a little yelp of delight and ran out, tail wagging furiously. She ran right up and jumped up at the person to say hello. The figure never moved. The dog grabbed hold of its sleeve and pulled it towards the chimney.

Tam watched in horror as they got close. It was a woman. She was dressed in an old overcoat with a string around the middle and rags tied round her under the coat. The big lump on her neck was a felted blob of greasy grey hair, a great lump of hair that looked as if it had never been washed or combed and which seemed to be part of her flesh. All down one side of her face the flesh was twisted and malformed with scars from some injury long ago. Her head hung to one side like a dead thing, her eyes stared – at the stones, at the ground, at the dog, at the sky, as if it was all the same. Her eyes were vacant but Tam sensed that her whole being was aware of him standing before her, and that he would die of fear if she looked straight at him.

This was no ghost. It was a tramp, a mad woman. An old bag lady.

The dog led her right up to Tam and stood there proudly, tail wagging. She seemed to be trying to introduce the two. Tam was disgusted. What a horrible old woman – he couldn't believe that she was anything to do with this bright dog. He pushed past her and ran out into the rain.

'Come on, girl, come on!' he shouted, clapping his hands. The dog just stood and looked at him. 'Come on, Winnie, come on – quick!' he shouted again. The dog glanced up at the old woman, licked her lips, turned in a circle – and sat down at her feet.

Tam was furious. How could the dog prefer that old creature to him? He ran halfway up the slope and turned back to look. The dog had forgotten him already. She was pulling the old woman into the chimney by the sleeve as if she were the pet and the dog her owner.

Tam was full of hatred for that old woman who had taken the dog away from him. She was barely human, she stank, she couldn't even dress herself properly. She was useless and old and horrible but the dog wanted her and Tam hated her for it.

He screamed at her through the rain, 'Go away!' She turned. She seemed to be looking along the valley but Tam was sure she had her eyes secretly on him.

'We don't want you here!' he shouted. The old woman's attention wandered and she began to turn away. The dog was looking curiously at him, her head cocked to one side.

Tam reached down and picked up a stone. He didn't know at whom he was throwing it, but his arm swung back and he sent the stone through the air towards them. It clattered in the chimney breast and bounced harmlessly onto the ground. The old woman turned towards the noise.

But the dog minded. Her lips went back. There was a choked noise – half bark, half growl. She ran swiftly across the fields straight at Tam.

Tam screamed and fled. He slithered up the slope, rushing and falling in the mud. He was halfway up the stone wall of the next field before he dared look back. The dog stood to attention in the rain staring after him twenty metres away. As Tam stood gasping for breath she turned her back on him and returned to the ruins where the old woman crouched under the chimney breast. Tam began to trudge slowly across the sodden fields back home.

Half an hour later he stood dripping on the kitchen floor. He didn't dare go right inside. He was in such a mess he felt proud of it and stood there leaking black water onto the clean kitchen floor.

'This is for me, is it?' demanded his mother. Tam grimaced and looked out of the window. It wasn't like that – was it?

'Take off your clothes and go up and have a bath.'

Tam sullenly began to undress. She watched him for a moment and then went up. He heard the bath being run. Then she came down and flung him an old towel.

'Well, don't just leave them there, put them in the machine,' she said as he stepped out of the pile of dirty clothes.

'You don't want to help, do you?' demanded his mother as he left the room. Tam said nothing.

## Chapter 2

Thowt It had been a private place for him but now Tam felt like an intruder. It was the little girl who belonged there; he was a ghost who spoiled her evenings by the fire. And there was the mad woman and her fierce, faithful dog. Where did they belong? Tam began to see the old woman about the town – standing in corners, picking through waste bins and rubbish, or just drifting along the streets. Her eyes were always down, in the gutter, unfocused, but she may have cast him one of those odd sideways glances when he looked away. Once he turned round and she was smiling at him – a toothless idiot's grin. It didn't seem to matter to her that she filled him with disgust. She didn't even seem to know.

A couple of days after he had appeared dripping on his mother's kitchen floor, Mrs Caradine collared him for one of her 'little chats'. She was a Health Visitor and had been friends with Tam's mother for a while on and off. Since his father went away she had been round all the time. It wasn't just friendship. Mrs Caradine loved doing good.

Tam was on his way home from school when she passed him in her car. She pulled over, wound down the window and gave him a big toothy smile.

'Fancy a lift, Tam? I'm going your way.'

'Thanks, it's all right.'

'I want to have a little chat. Come on – jump in ...'

He only lived a minute away. She wasn't an aunt or anything, not even a very good friend. She didn't start the car when he climbed in but got stuck straight in.

'I know it's none of my business,' she began – that's what she always said.

'I know,' Tam interrupted. 'My mum.'

'You could help a little more.'

He shrugged. 'I do my chores.'

'She says ...' Mrs Caradine stopped short when she saw Tam pull a face.

'Well, what does she say?' he demanded.

'She wouldn't want me telling tales,' said Mrs Caradine, smiling cautiously. 'I know things aren't so easy at home. It's hard for her, Tam – holding down a morning job, looking after the house – and you. She hasn't got a lot of time but it's not her fault. It happens – families split up. She didn't want it, you know ...'

Tam knew that. He'd heard them downstairs going over it, and over and over it. She hadn't wanted it.

'You could help a bit more,' repeated Mrs Caradine. 'And there's school. You keep getting into trouble.'

'How do you know that?'

'They've been ringing up home. Didn't you know?'

Tam didn't know and Mrs Caradine got all flustered. 'Me and my big mouth,' she moaned.

'I'd just prefer to live with my dad, that's all,' said Tam.

'Would you? Why don't you?'

Tam began to explain abut the little flat in

Bradford with Julia's children all over the place and no room for him. Mrs Caradine listened sympathetically.

'And there you are stuck with your poor old mum while your dad's off having a good time, is that it?'

Tam grinned and nodded. That's how it felt, but it wasn't like that. He'd spent a couple of weekends in Bradford and even he had to admit it was better at home.

'I can't see what's so great about Julia and her family,' complained Tam.

'It sounds as if it's your dad you're angry at,' remarked Mrs Caradine, 'and your mum just gets it in the neck – right?'

That was about it.

She started up the car and drove off, talking about working it out together and new routines now his dad was gone and so on. Tam nodded and looked out of the window. He'd heard it before.

Tam had already had enough. He was fed up with being in trouble, fed up with arguments no one could win. In his heart he wasn't even sure he'd prefer to live with his dad. He certainly didn't want to live in Bradford.

Mrs Caradine was still rattling away as she pulled up outside his house, but she stopped in mid-flow.

'Look,' she said.

It was the beggar woman. She was standing by the entrance to the cricket club, a hunched bundle of rags with two swollen polythene bags in her hands. A small band of kids were standing around jeering.

Mrs Caradine leapt into action. 'What are you doing? Why can't you be nice to her? Can't you see she needs help?' she shouted. She climbed out of the car and ran across the road. The kids scattered and stopped to watch from a safe distance. Mrs Caradine went up to the old woman and bent down, holding her arm and talking to her. The old woman looked anxious. Her gaze drifted up and down the road as if she were trapped in some deep, unhappy thought. But Tam could see the whites of her eyes as she glanced towards him. Mrs Caradine was gesturing towards the house and she began to pull at her sleeves. The old woman let herself be pulled by the arm across the road.

'What're you doing to her?' said Tam. It seemed so unfair; the old woman was miserable enough and now Mrs Caradine was frightening her.

'A cup of tea and a bite to eat, I'm sure your mum won't mind,' beamed Mrs Caradine, as happy as a hamster in a wheel now that she had a good deed to do.

Tam hurried across the pavement to open the door. He forgot about the plight of the bag lady. The last thing he wanted was that old hag in his house.

'Mum!' She came along the corridor and peered around the door. Tam pointed and rolled his eyes.

'Good grief, who's she got this time – her grandmother?' hissed his mother. Tam grinned. But his mother was waving to Mrs Caradine.

'Hello, Helen – I've brought a visitor for you,' called Mrs Caradine.

'But she stinks,' whispered Tam. 'She'll have fleas and things. We could catch something.'

'I can't stop her, you know what she's like,' whispered his mother back, still smiling away. 'Go and put the kettle on. And put newspapers on the armchairs in case she wants to sit down. It's a good job we haven't got any family silver,' she added, and she stepped out to give Mrs Caradine a hand.

Close up, perched on a piece of newspaper on the edge of one of the armchairs in the clean sitting room, the old woman looked filthier and more pitiful than ever. She was unwashed, uncombed, unloved. The scar on her face looked raw and red under the dirt. To Tam it was as if a disease had come to sit in his living room. She had black, greasy lines around her eyes and mouth and her eyes looked sore and red against the dark skin. Her hair hung in wads, like felted cloth down to her shoulders. She gazed down at the carpet, but every muscle in her was tight. She didn't seem to be aware of anything, least of all Mrs Caradine.

Mrs Caradine was crouching by her side, all elegant in a smart green suit, smiling up at her alarmed old face and trying to get some sense out of her. But the beggar woman just held on to the sides of the chair as if it was doing a hundred miles an hour and didn't say a word. Tam and his mother had taken refuge in the kitchen.

'You should have put paper on the arms, she must be crawling,' moaned his mother. She was hurtling round the kitchen, making tea, cutting bread, frying bacon for a buttie. She loved this sort of situation where she could rush about making clever remarks.

'Where's the butter?' she demanded desperately, slopping the milk as she poured it into the cups.

'Use marg,' suggested Tam.

'No, no give her the best,' she insisted. She found

it in the fridge and began scraping rapidly at it to make it soft.

Tam peered around the door. Mrs Caradine wasn't making much progress. 'You can get typhoid off fleas,' he pointed out. 'The Black Death. I bet we all get bitten.'

'Mrs Caradine's probably immune to the Black Death,' suggested his mother.

'Mrs Caradine probably is the Black Death,' said Tam.

They smiled at each other. It was like old times.

Mrs Caradine got stiffly to her feet, smiling kindly.

'Poor old thing, she's terrified,' murmured his mother, peering through the crack in the door over Tam's shoulder. Mrs Caradine had two smiles – a nice one when she forgot herself and a professional, extra-kind one, when she was doing her job. 'She probably keeps an entirely different face in a jar by the door for when she gets home,' muttered his mother, slapping the bread together.

Tam stared through at the mysterious old woman. She stared right back at him. He had the sickening feeling the old woman expected him to do something for her. As if that meeting on the hill meant something – as if he knew her – as if he was anything to do with her. Mrs Caradine, smiling and chatting above her head, didn't seem to notice anything.

Tam would have banged the door shut but his mother paused and had another peek over his shoulder before going in.

'I wonder what happened to her face?' she murmured. She glanced at her son and kissed him suddenly. 'Who's she got to love her?' she asked, and she went in, bearing bacon butties and tea.

'I can't get a word out of her,' announced Mrs Caradine. Tam's mother bent down with the plate of sandwiches.

'Would you like a butty?' she said in a loud voice, as if the old woman were deaf.

'Go on, Rosey – take one,' urged Mrs Caradine. The old woman's hand began to drift up to the plate. She stared vaguely at the carpet as if the hand was acting all on its own – as if it belonged to someone else altogether and she knew nothing of its comings and goings. Her hand took the sandwich and put it inside her coat.

'Saving it for later,' said Mrs Caradine wisely.

'Is that her name – Rosey?' asked Tam.

Mrs Caradine shrugged. 'That's what those children were calling her – Rosey Rubbish,' she said apologetically. 'She won't tell me her real name, but Rosey's as nice as anything, don't you think?'

'Have another sandwich, Rosey,' said Tam's mother holding out the plate. Once again the hand stole secretly out. She tucked the sandwich with the other one under her coat.

'She's a big eater,' said Tam's mum.

Mrs Caradine had to dash off. Before she went she rang the police and spent another unsuccessful five minutes trying to get some information out of Rosey.

'Another victim of "back into the community",' she said as she put her coat on. 'Dumping people out on the streets, more like it.' She paused and looked down at the dirty grey head. ' Poor thing – I wonder how she ended up like this ... Did you see that programme a few weeks ago,' she went on, 'about a girl who got pregnant and her parents put her away in a mental home and she stayed there for fifty years even though there was nothing wrong with her? Those homes in the 40s and 50s were no better than prisons. People locked up all day with nothing to do – treated like idiots ... And of course after forty or fifty years of that – well, look at her. No nice safe locked room, no medication – having to cope for herself and she can't. So much for progress,' added Mrs Caradine sarcastically. 'Then we used to lock them up and let them rot; now we just leave them to rot on the street. Well, I must dash. Thank you so much for taking her in, Helen!' Mrs Caradine administered a smile. 'The police will take her off your hands. At least she'll get a hot meal down her and a bed for the night.' She smiled again and left.

Mrs Sams saw Mrs Caradine to the door and went to make another butty, leaving Tam standing awkwardly in front of Rosey. She seemed to have forgotten him now and was staring down at the floor. Just the sight of her, her skin, the dirt, the wrongness of her, made him feel sick.

That night Tam thought of the old lady under the ground in the police cells. He thought that if he were her he'd prefer to sleep out in the open, out under the chimney stack at Thowt It Farm, or in a barn or a shed if it was raining. He remembered how the old woman had looked in the house – her eyes wide and frightened. She looked so much more miserable inside, somehow. Just as the police has been leading her out she had held out an arm towards Tam. Her gaze came up – not to his face but to one side of it, and her mouth began to work as if she had something to say but couldn't get it out.

'Goodbye,' said Tam.

Her expression changed. Her mouth moved from a circle of disappointment into a faint half smile, a pale, old ghost of a smile, before it all collapsed and she let herself be led out passively into the police car.

# Chapter 3

'Good Lord ...' His mother peered into his suitcase. She took out the clothes he had stuffed in and started to fold them properly. 'You've got enough for a fortnight here. You are planning on coming back, aren't you?' she asked brightly.

Tam was cross. 'Don't make stupid jokes.'

'I'm sorry.' She smacked herself on the hand. 'You've been a sweetie lately. I know it's not been easy.'

'It's all his fault,' said Tam savagely.

'Now, now.' She peered over the suitcase lid at him. 'We just have to get on with it, Tam.'

Tam slouched over to the window. Having decided that his mother wasn't to blame he'd begun to hate his dad. He had to trek all that way just to see his own father. 'Do I have to go?' he growled.

She raised her eyebrows. 'I never thought about it. Don't you want to?'

Tam shrugged. 'Why can't he come to see me here?'

His mother looked away and twisted her mouth. 'I don't think that would be a good idea,' she said grimly. 'Anyway, you'd better make up your mind. He'll be here in a couple of hours.'

'I suppose I'd better go,' said Tam.

'Poor Tam!' She looked sympathetically at him. 'First you hate me and then you hate him. It'll settle down.'

Tam smiled wryly. He glanced out of his window. Lying across the sky the hill lay dappled in sunshine, unmoved by his troubles.

'I'm going to go out for a bit,' Tam said. 'I'll be back before he comes.' He left the room and grabbed his coat. If he was going to be stuck in that poky little flat with those ghastly kids all weekend, he'd get a bit of outside now while he still could.

Tam went down the track that led past the cricket club and the allotments to the little bridge where people took their children to feed the ducks. The hill that hid Thowt It rose immediately above him, but he didn't want to go up. He hadn't been back yet. It was a secret that he wished he didn't know but that he wished he could know better. Whenever he saw the old woman he felt a secret thrill of fascination. He had seen mad things and met a mad woman on the hill. Was she a witch? Or was he like her?

He ran past the willow hedge by the allotments. The smooth, yellow branches were covered in long buds. Little yellow flowers pushed their way past last year's dead stems. It was April – a cold, still, bright day.

Where the bridge crossed the stream there was a hole knocked in the wall for the younger kids to peep through and see the ducks and geese. Tam could see over the top, but he liked to lean through the hole and watch the silly things look anxiously up for bread. He had nothing. He spat in the water and they all came rushing forward excitedly and then floated in circles wondering where the bread had gone. A mother duck with a little fleet of tiny ducklings appeared, bobbing rapidly up and down in the water – eight, nine, ten, he counted, and there were more, but they bobbed to and fro so much he couldn't count them any more.

A dog barked right behind him. Startled, Tam banged his head and he banged it again trying to get out quickly. He was scared of a bite in his pants but the bark wasn't angry. There she was – Winnie from Thowt It Farm. She seemed to have forgotten that they'd had an argument. She was sitting right up next to him, begging and cocking her ears brightly and ludicrously and wagging her tail.

'Good girl ...' Tam was wary. He rubbed her ears and patted her. She seemed real enough – rather smelly, even, as if she'd been rolling in something.

The dog licked his hands. 'Have you come down to town for the day?' asked Tam, glancing up at the ridge. As if she read his thoughts Winnie jumped up and ran a little way along the path that led up to Thowt It. She stopped, whining, looking back at Tam.

'Where's Rosey?' he asked. The dog cocked her head. Maybe that wasn't the old woman's name after all.

Winnie barked again and ran excitedly backwards and forwards. She looked over her shoulder at him. Tam looked back to his house. He had a couple of hours. He followed her up the slope.

Winnie was as busy and funny as ever. She kept finding imaginary rabbits in the grass and getting excited and then finding they weren't there. When she saw some rooks poking their beaks in the ground a field away she shot off, straining forward after them. Of course they saw her coming a mile off and just flapped lazily into the air. But she was pleased with herself anyway and came back wagging her tail proudly to be congratulated. Tam threw some sticks for her to chase on the way. She could leap right up and snatch them out of the air with her teeth.

Tam almost forgot where they were going, but then the ruined farm suddenly popped into sight – Who'd-a-thought-it? – just like its name. He stopped and scanned the ruins. There was no one to be seen. Had a dog called Winnie lived there years ago? Tam decided to ask someone more about the farm.

He followed her around the broken walls, encouraging her to find some rabbits. When they got bored with that Tam searched around for another stick to throw. But before he found one he heard the dog whine excitedly and bark.

He knew she'd come. Tam felt a delicious, frightened shiver down his spine. The mad woman was back.

She was standing by a low wall near the chimney, not looking at him but away along the hillside – not looking at anything, just standing there for nothing. But she knew he was there. Tam was certain.

The dog ran up and pawed at her. She looked down and her hand drifted, drifted like a lost soul down to its head. Winnie licked the hand and looked expectantly at Tam.

'Hello,' he said. The old woman's eyes moved but she said nothing. Winnie barked.

Tam decided to make an effort. He put out his hand and said, 'I'm Tam, how do you do?' But he didn't want her to touch him. The dog thumped the short turf with her tail. The old woman turned slightly. She didn't put out her hand or look at him but she tipped her head to one side and the slightest little smile flowered on her withered mouth.

'She's a lovely dog,' said Tam enthusiastically. 'Is she yours?' The old woman looked doubtfully at Winnie and then at Tam. She lifted her chin in the air and looked slightly indignant; Tam thought maybe she had stolen her.

There was an awkward pause. 'I'm Tam,' said Tam again. 'What's your name?'

The mad woman frowned. She pursed her lips and moved her mouth. Nothing came out.

'Is it Rosey? Rosey's a nice name,' said Tam. The old woman turned her face to the ground and her mouth took on its familiar oval of unhappiness.

Tam was bored. She wasn't frightening after all – nor even mysterious once you tried to talk to her – just dull and stupid. Just a miserable old woman who didn't know what was what. He was glad he'd talked to her just to find out she was nothing after all. But he didn't like her any better.

'Where do you sleep?' he asked suddenly. He was thinking that he could tell Mrs Caradine and have the old woman taken away again. If they did take her away, maybe they'd leave the dog behind. Besides, she needed to be put somewhere, she wasn't safe out in this weather, she'd catch her death...

The old woman's mouth opened a little; she appeared to be thinking. Tam felt excited; surely he was about to make a discovery. The dog wanted to help, too. She sat upright with her ears cocked and looked so intelligent that you felt you could almost hold a conversation with her. And then Winnie began to move her head up and down in that curious way. 'Yes, yes, yes, yes, yes ...'

Rosey seemed to make up her mind. She smiled at him, a flash of expression in her unhappy grey face, and then turned and began to walk around the wall into the remains of the room with the chimney. When she got to the old fireplace she glanced at him out of the corner of her eyes; he could see the whites of her eyes flashing as she did it. She stood still, nodding at the grass.

'In the fireplace?' asked Tam. 'That can't be very warm. I'm sure we could find something better.' He bent down to peer in. Behind him the dog came up and gave him a nose in his back. Tam did as he was told and went forward under the chimney.

It was cold. Something seemed to be sliding over him, or through him. Then he thought he must be falling and his hands flew out to the brick wall to stop his head from bumping, but he twisted and seemed to miss the ground altogether. He cried out.

Then it stopped. He was unexpectedly on his backside on solid ground. He had his hands stretched out and his face pulled back. The wall that had been in front was now behind him. He was in a farmyard. There were chickens pecking and a strong smell of straw and manure. Tam backed into the wall; he was terrified, he felt sick. Everything had gone wrong. He had been moved out of his place – but then he saw that it was the same place. There above him was the old familiar hill, just as it had been a moment before, lying in the same secret stillness. But then he saw it was not the same, not quite. It was purple, but he had seen it like this before.

The heather was out. The leaves were turning. Spring had gone and it was autumn – a blowy autumn day with big fluffy clouds and yellow leaves scutting about the yard. And there were the Scots pines, but now in a dense thicket of shrubs with young saplings around them. Winnie was standing by his side; she barked twice and sat down. She seemed to be smiling. But Tam felt really dizzy – he was all wrong, he shouldn't be here. Had he gone mad?

He noticed Rosey standing by him. He was sure she hadn't been there before. He turned on her.

'Where are we?' he demanded. She said nothing. Her mouth was working and she was nodding her head. She had that faint smile again. For a second Tam thought she was laughing at him.

'What have you done to me?' he shouted.

The old woman looked blankly past him.

'You ... What have you done?' demanded Tam in a frightened rage. He would have jumped at her and screamed, but the dog was near and watching him closely.

This was her place. He *had* gone mad – just like the old woman. She had taken him to a place where mad people go.

Then he heard the most awful noise – a grunting, squealing, groaning noise. Something dreadful was coming. He looked for somewhere to hide ... and an enormous spotty pig came galloping round the side of the house. On its back was perched a small girl. She had a tight grip on the pig's ears and she was bouncing up and down, squealing with delight – squealing almost as loudly as the pig. The pig charged round and round in circles, roaring and grunting and squealing and bucking like a fat, pink, bald pony, with the little girl hanging on for dear life. Her hair flapped up and down and she was shouting, 'Yippie, ride 'em, ride 'em,' in a funny, high voice. The whole thing looked so ridiculous that despite himself, Tam burst out laughing.

The girl looked up in surprise. The pig kicked out its back legs like a bronco and flung its back up. She was catapulted head over heels onto a pile of mud in the corner. That is, it looked like mud, but you could never be sure, not in a farmyard.

Tam stopped laughing. The girl sat up, covered in straw and muck. She stared at him. The dog went over to laugh at her and sniff around her, but she pushed her away. She stood up, still staring. Her look was so strange and intense that Tam was frightened of her. She began to circle around him, examining him from tip to toe as if he were an animal in the zoo. Tam glanced down at himself. Everything seemed as usual. He felt panicky. He looked to one side to see if he could see the way back, but there was nothing, nothing that was not of this other world. He felt a strange fizzy sensation bubbling up in his tummy, like a shaken-up bottle of lemonade. He thought he might suddenly shoot his cork off the top of his head. He was scared stiff but he felt like giggling.

'I must be hysterical,' he said to himself. 'Stop it, Tam, stop it.' But it didn't go away.

The girl came closer. 'Who are you?' she

demanded. 'What are you doing on my farm?'

'I think I'm lost,' said Tam.

This seemed to make an impression on the girl. She had to think about it and then at last she put her hands on her hips and said firmly, 'Did you ever ride a pig?'

Tam said, 'No.' He was glancing from side to side, sure that the whole scene would disappear at any second.

'Would you like to ride one?' demanded the girl.

There was nothing for it. He might be mad but here he was, for the time being at least. Tam shrugged and said, 'Yes, please.'

'Come on then!' The girl clapped her hands and called to the pig: 'Here, Spot, here, Spot ...'

Tam giggled. The fizzy bubbly feeling was so strong that he thought that if he started laughing now he'd never stop. He tried to bite his lip but it was no good and he began to spill over into gurgling laughter.

'What's the matter?' demanded the girl.

'Spot – is that your pig's name? It's a funny name for a pig, isn't it?' he babbled. 'What do you call your dog?' he giggled. 'Porky?' And he began spluttering with laughter.

The girl looked at him for a second in surprise. She had a think about it and then she began to laugh too. 'Porky – that's a silly name for a dog,' she giggled.

'Not as silly as ... as ... as ...' But he couldn't speak any more.

'Not as silly as Spot for a pig,' finished the girl for him. And they both began screaming with laughter, even though it wasn't that funny – spluttering and screaming until they fell over and rolled about in the dust and straw. Winnie thought it was a new game and joined in, growling and pulling at their clothes and making the whole thing even funnier. Eventually they had to lie on the ground biting the inside of their mouths to stop the funniness of the whole thing bubbling out of them all over again.

At last the girl got up. 'You're funny,' she said. Tam nodded. He wasn't normally funny, but he was now. 'My name's May,' said the girl.

'I'm Tam.'

'Do you live here now, like me?' she wanted to know – as if he could start living somewhere just by turning up. But he was lost here. He glanced around for Rosey. She was standing to one side watching them out of the corner of her eye.

'I... I don't know,' he said.

'You can if you want,' said the girl. 'Now – Spot! Spotty Pig! Where are you?' The pig looked up from where it had been rooting about in the straw and came trotting over, just as if she really were a dog. She grunted and butted May a couple of times, while she shrieked at it to stay still. She began patting it – whacking it, really – until great clouds of dried mud rose from her skin and Spot closed her eyes and grunted contentedly.

'Spot's the best horsey ever,' announced May. Tam nearly began giggling again – first it was a pig dog, now it was a horse pig – but he bit his tongue and watched as May clambered on its back.

'Come on – you get behind me,' shouted May. Tam crawled on behind her. Spot was broad and warm and not very clean. He was in his good clothes but he didn't care. Maybe he'd wake up in a minute. The skin was hard and rough and warm and had lots of long, wispy, stiff hairs growing out of it. Tam scratched her back. Spot seemed to like it and relaxed and grunted.

'Go!' shouted May. The pig bounded forward suddenly and Tam fell off.

'Not much good, are you?' she shouted gleefully.

There was more to riding a pig than met the eye. The next time he leant across the girl and held the pig's ears like she did. He held the tops of them, she held the bottoms. He still only managed to stay on for a half a minute, but he got better and better every time.

Tam hadn't had so much fun for ages. The pig careered and cantered round and round the farmyard, banging into walls, kicking and leaping about in the air to try and get them off. Spot was a big pig; time and time again they both shot off up into the air and thudded onto the hard ground. But there was no time to be sorry because you had to try and catch up and clamber back on. Chickens and ducks flapped and screeched, trying to get out of the way. Winnie barked and tried to jump on but she never could and so she tried to catch the old pig by the tail instead. The rooster got so cross he flew onto her back and tried to peck his way through her skin. But the pig's skin was tough and she just closed her eyes and grunted happily.

At last Spot sank down to the ground. The two children jumped on top of her and banged their heels and shouted, but she just refused to budge. May sighed.

'That means she's had enough,' she explained.

They got off and Spot rolled over onto her back, waving her trotters in the air. May flung herself down, dug in her fingernails and gave the pig a good hard scratch.

'Come on – she likes it.' Tam joined in and they thanked the pig the way she liked best, with a good, long, hard scratch.

Everything went quiet. The chickens started clucking and pecking. Winnie rolled over and began bathing in the dust and Spot the pig lay back and groaned blissfully, her little pink eyes closing up and her wet snout quivering in the air. Just watching her made Tam feel tired. They scratched and scratched with fingers and sticks and little stones until at last the pig keeled over sideways and fell asleep with a long sigh. He and May lay back against her big hot belly. The sun was warm, the sound of the farmyard soothing ...

There was a step behind them. A man's voice: 'Well I'm glad you're softening her up again. She'll be as tough as old boots after all that running about.'

Tam looked up. It was a tall, wide man with white hair and a red face. He was dressed in a pair of great trousers tied around his waist with string, big brown boots and a tatty black coat. May got up and walked away towards the barn with her nose in the air when she saw him.

The man laughed at her. 'Don't worry, May – Spot's our pet, aren't you, old girl? We wouldn't eat her – I couldn't get her down.' He bent slowly down and tickled the pig under the chin. Then he stood up and gave her a hefty kick with his boot. Spot grunted indignantly – she seemed just too big to be hurt – and scrambled to her feet. 'Go on, clear off, go and stuff your face, you're not fat enough,' he told her. Spot snuffled the air, shook herself down and wandered off in the direction of the orchard to look for windfall apples.

The old man turned and looked carefully at Tam. 'Well,' he said. 'That were a lark, weren't it? You'd best come in and have a bite and a glass o' milk.'

Tam looked around for May. She was walking away into the barn with Winnie on her heels. He suddenly wanted badly to go home, but the old woman had vanished too. Could he get back on his own? He hesitated, not knowing what to do.

'You come with me,' ordered the man. 'Don't worry about May – she'll come in her own time. Come on – smartish-like!'

Tam followed him into the house.

# Chapter 4

The farmer led him into a stone-flagged kitchen. There was an enormous black metal fireplace with hotplates and an oven built into it. Even though it was warm outside there was a coal fire burning, suspended above the ground behind a six-barred grate. The walls were all painted white. There was a long wooden table surrounded by six chairs, a big armchair pushed against the wall and a square clock with one hand tick-tocking on the wall.

The old man turned to stare at him. 'What's yer name?' he demanded.

'Tam.'

The farmer held out his hand. 'Nutter,' he said.

'What ...?'

'My name – Sam Nutter!'

Tam shook the big hard hand.

'Now then, Tam. How long is it since you had bacon and eggs?'

In fact Tam had bacon and eggs every Saturday for breakfast. But the old man said it in such a way – as if he were offering some sort of wonderful treasure.

'Ages!' exclaimed Tam. It seemed the right response.

The old man nodded. 'Right.' He took a cast-iron frying pan down from a nail on the wall and put it on the stove. Then he went to the pantry and came back with eggs, a big hunk of fatty bacon, and a loaf of bread with a thick, burned crust. He began cutting slices of bacon on the table casting little glances over his shoulder at Tam as he did so.

Tam glanced anxiously at the door. 'Is May coming in?' he asked.

'In her own time,' said Mr Nutter comfortably. 'Sit yerself down, lad. Don't stand there like a bowl of spare custard.'

Tam sat at the table, which was very high and made him feel unpleasantly small. He knew what was coming next. Questions. Whatever would he say?

'Staying down in Cawldale, are yer?' asked the man, shooting Tam a glance from under his frizzy eyebrows.

'That's right,' said Tam. He was feeling excited, light-headed. It was like being a spy – a spy from another world.

'Not from these parts, are you?'

Tam knew the answer to that one. He had moved up from London a few years ago and he still had a southern accent. 'Down South,' he answered. 'London.'

Mr Nutter snorted as if London were some sort of disease. He glanced back. 'Evacuee?' he demanded.

'That's it,' said Tam, who wasn't sure what the word meant. The farmer flung three thick slices of bacon in the pan where they began to sizzle slowly. A delicious smell filled the room and Tam's mouth began to water.

'Mam and Dad?' he demanded.

'Dead,' said Tam, with great relish.

To his surprise the old man turned round to stare at him, his big flat face looking astonished, his eyebrows up in his hair. Then he turned abruptly and wandered off to a corner under the old clock. He stood there all hunched up for a moment staring gloomily at the skirting and took out a large handkerchief and blew his nose wetly. When he came back his clear blue eyes had gone red and wet. The old man had been crying. Tam felt guilty for his fib.

'Bloody war,' growled the farmer. He suddenly took an enormous kick at the iron range. The range must have weighed a ton because it just clunked softly. The frying pan didn't so much as shiver and the bacon sizzled comfortably on. The farmer groaned and clutched his toe.

'You damned thing,' he cried in pain. He sat down to nurse his foot and nodded at the stove in admiration. 'That old stove's the only thing tough enough in here for kicking at,' he said. 'I've given it hell for fifty year and it don't even know it.' Tam saw that the stove was covered with marks where the old man had kicked it across the years. But it didn't have a single dent.

What with playing with May and Spot and smelling the bacon cooking, Tam was ravenous by the time the meal was ready. Mr Nutter put out two fat slices of bacon for himself and one for Tam, with an egg each and a slab of thick bread. On May's plate there was just bread and two eggs.

'May likes pigs too much to eat 'em,' he explained. 'Pity she don't like pigs a bit less and folk a bit more,' he added. 'Do you like dripping?' Tam wasn't at all sure what dripping was. He glanced at the tap, but the old man nodded and smiled to himself as if the answer was obvious. He held the frying pan over

Tam's plate and poured a thick stream of hot fat over it, until the food was lying in a puddle of fat. Tam stared. His mother would have been disgusted.

'Get that down yer,' growled the farmer. 'Don't wait for us.' He stood over Tam watching him closely as he cut off a corner of the bacon and popped it in.

It was the strangest bacon he had ever tasted. He couldn't quite place it at first, but after a few chews he realised what it was. It tasted the way Spotty Pig smelt; it tasted of pigs. He didn't mention it, though, for fear of being rude.

'Wonderful!' he exclaimed.

Mr Nutter nodded in satisfaction and banged the frying pan violently on the table.

'May! Grub!' he bellowed. He sat down, picked up his knife and fork, which looked like toys in his enormous red hands, and began carefully cutting up his bacon.

Tam looked at him as he ate. He had a big flat red face with white hair and a pair of watery blue eyes which were wide open, as if he'd seen a ghost. They were still wet from where he had cried. When he saw Tam looking he pointed his fork at Tam's plate.

'Eat,' he ordered.

Tam ate. He had never had bacon and eggs like it. Once you got used to the fact that the bacon tasted of pigs it got more and more delicious. It was over a centimetre thick and nearly half of it was fat, singed brown in the pan. Tam started cutting the fat off, but he saw the old man chop it into chunks and eat it. Fat was obviously something special, so he popped a lump cautiously in. It was sweet and chewy. Tam gobbled it up and mopped up the puddle of fat on his plate with the bread crust. Mr Nutter nodded approvingly.

The milk was different, too. He took a long drink and pulled a face.

'Wassamarra!' demanded the old man, who was watching him like a hawk. 'Fresh this morning, that is.'

'It ... it tastes of cows,' said Tam.

Mr Nutter's eyebrows shot up into his hair. 'Of course it tastes of cows, yer daft 'appeth – it comes out of one. Do you think the fairies bring it round in bottles? Londoners,' he muttered to himself, and shook his head sadly.

Tam took another swig. It was creamy enough, but he didn't really like it.

All the time they were eating May's place remained empty. The farmer didn't seem to worry about it and he just waved his fork in the air when Tam mentioned it. But halfway through, he leaned across and pointed at May's plate.

A small, brown hand was coming up from underneath the table. The hand was groping about in the middle of the plate, getting deplorably fatty and yolky. Finally it managed to pile the eggs in between the bread – not easy when you aren't looking – and then disappeared under the table. A second later May crept out from under the table on two knees and one hand, holding her double egg sandwich in the other. She was concentrating very hard on not dropping anything but she was still leaving a trail of yolk and fat behind her. After her came Winnie, licking the floor clean as she went. Every now and then she gave May a good, hard push with her nose. She was trying to make her drop the eggs.

Mr Nutter winked at Tam. He bent right down under the table until his head was almost upside down. When she got to the door, which she opened with her chin, May glanced back and was greeted by the sight of Mr Nutter's astonished face, redder than ever, staring upside down at her across the flags. May screamed. She jumped up, snatched one of her eggs, flung it at his head and ran out of the room. Mr Nutter made no attempt to dodge but her aim was bad and the egg splattered on the table leg. Tam jumped up just in time to see her run across the yard and hide in the dog kennel by the gate. Meanwhile, Winnie licked the floor and the table clean of egg, wagged her tail at Mr Nutter and Tam and hurried off after her.

'I normally pay no notice of it,' explained Mr Nutter. He raised his eyebrows and methodically began to chop up another piece of bacon.

'Does she do that often?' asked Tam.

'Oh, aye, most often,' replied the farmer calmly.

'Aren't you going to do anything?'

The farmer scratched his ear with his fork. 'Do anything? Like punish her, you mean? No, nothing at all. Not but that I can't be strict if I want to,' he added, pointing his knife significantly at Tam. 'But sometimes it's best to turn a blind eye. She's had her fair share of troubles, May has. Mind you,' he added wistfully, 'I'm looking forward to the day when I can give her a good hiding for her manners. She's earned it.' He returned to his bacon, and Tam didn't ask any more.

When he had finished his meal, Mr Nutter put down his knife and fork and began firing more questions at Tam. When had he arrived, how had he travelled, how long was he staying, where was he staying ...? Tam did his best, but he wasn't sure he was believed. He told the old man vaguely that he had only arrived that day and couldn't remember the name of the road or the family he was staying with.

'Not too good at remembering, are yer?' growled the old man. Then he wanted to know about Tam's clothes, which he seemed to think were something exotic, although Tam only had jeans, anorak and trainers on.

'What sort of stuff is it, anyhow?' he asked, feeling the nylon part of the anorak with his fingers. 'Some sort of substitute?'

'Something like that,' said Tam.

'Don't look none too warm,' said Mr Nutter, frowning suspiciously.

After there was apple pie. Mr Nutter cut him a fat slice and topped it with thick cream. 'My bacon, my eggs, my apples, my cream, my butter,' he said proudly.

'Gosh,' said Tam, impressed. He took a mouthful. 'It's lovely,' he said. 'Did your wife make it?'

Mr Nutter shook his head. 'Mrs Nutter's been gone seven year. I get a lady in to do it. Mrs Pickles can't make pie like my Martha did.' He shook his head sorrowfully and winked. 'Which is just as well, because my Martha were the worst cook in Yorkshire. Pastry like lead. But I still miss her. I'd rather have my Martha back than marry Mrs Pickles, soggy pastry and all,' he declared. He drooped sadly in his chair at the thought of his Martha, all damp-eyed again. Then he picked up and banged the table.

'May! Puddin'!' he yelled.

He sat down to eat and the whole thing happened again. May crept in on her hands and knees and stole her own dinner. Again Mr Nutter bent down so that she glanced back from the door and saw his face peering upside down at her.

She screamed and snatched at her pie.

'That's the last slice, mind,' said the farmer quickly. 'There'll be no more if tha throws that.'

May glared at him and ran out. Mr Nutter nodded happily. 'It'd break my heart seeing good pie going down that dog,' he said, and he took a huge spoonful of his.

Mr Nutter carefully wiped all the cream off his bowl with his pie crust. Then he pushed the bowl away and looked at Tam.

'Now then,' he said seriously. Tam was in for a talk. 'You can come here as often as you like and you can stay here as long as you like,' he said. 'You can help me if you like – or not, if you like. You can play wi' horses if you like, or wi' pigs or wi' chickens – if you like. You can play on haystacks or in barn. You can eat here if you like and you can sleep here if you like, and if Mrs Wot's-'er-name in Wotsit Road lets you, you can stay here if you like. Do I make myself clear?'

'Yes,' said Tam doubtfully. He was still waiting for the catch when the farmer leaned back and pushed himself up from the table.

'My May's taken a shine to you and that goes a long way in my books,' he said, getting up to put the kettle on. 'Cup o' tea for me. You run along and play wi' her – if you like.'

Tam glanced at the clock. Three o'clock. But what was the time in the real world – his world? He felt that every second that passed, every new thing that happened made this world more real and his world more shadowy. His dad would be waiting for him.

'I'd better be going,' he said.

Mr Nutter poured out a glass of milk. 'Gi' that to May before you go. She'll be in dog kennel. Don't mind her if she's cross, it's her way.'

Tam took the milk. He wanted to say something – to thank the farmer for being kind, to say that this little trip to another world had been wonderful.

'Thanks for the breakfast,' he said. Mr Nutter nodded.

She was in the dog kennel as Mr Nutter had said. She lay half in, half out on her tummy with Winnie on top of her. She crawled out when Tam came up and took the milk. She wasn't at all cross. She sat cross-legged in the dust to drink her milk. Tam sat down beside her.

May was a strange girl. She was two or three years younger than him with green, wide apart eyes and a scruff of short brown hair, full of straw and bits of twigs and terribly untidy. She was nut brown and had very strong, muscular little arms and legs, as Tam had found out when they were playing with the pig. She wore a short printed frock which was almost as dirty as she was. When she spoke she stared directly at him; it would have been rude in anyone else, but in her it didn't seem to matter. And she spoke in a funny high note that was squeaky and musical and a bit flat – as if her voice was out of practice, or as if she were a bit deaf.

Winnie came out of the kennel to lie across her legs, and the little girl buried her fingers in the thick fur of her neck and scratched her.

'She's a lovely dog,' said Tam.

May nodded. 'She rescued me,' she said. 'He called her Winnie after the Prime Minister,' she added nodding at the house.

Tam nodded. He'd never heard of a Prime Minister Winnie, but that meant nothing. 'How did she rescue you?' he asked.

May stared at him. 'You know,' she said.

Tam looked down. He didn't want to admit to her that he didn't know, that he knew nothing at all.

She was staring so hard at him that Tam was embarrassed and he looked away. But May wanted him to understand and she touched his face with her hand so that he had to look back. 'You're my first friend,' she said. 'You're the one lost like I was, so I love you.'

Tam blushed. Children didn't love one another, did they?

May smiled and leaned back against the kennel to sip her milk.

'Didn't you mind eating inside?' she asked.

'No.'

May frowned. 'I hate it inside,' she said at last. 'He wants me to eat in there but I won't.'

'Why not?' asked Tam.

She pulled a face. 'I hate it inside,' she repeated. 'I never go inside, except occasionally. Like that time I made toast,' she added. Tam looked at her. 'I knew you must be friendly when I saw Winnie was with you,' she explained. So that was why she had taken to him so quickly.

'Did you like him?' she said, nodding at the farmhouse again.

Tam hadn't been sure at first but now he was. 'Oh, yes – he's funny.'

May giggled. 'He stands on his head on the table sometimes when he wants to make me laugh,' she said.

Tam tried to imagine Mr Nutter upside down with his enormous boots in the air. He couldn't do it. 'He said I could visit here whenever I like. He's very generous, isn't he?'

But May frowned. 'You're not to visit,' she said. 'You live here. He's not to say that.'

'I have a place ...' began Tam.

'He's not to say that,' she insisted.

'He didn't say I couldn't live here,' said Tam.

'But your parents are dead,' she told him. She smiled proudly. 'I heard you telling him. I was listening.'

'But ...' Tam began.

May gazed hard at him. 'You were lying,' she said matter-of-factly.

Tam felt uncomfortable under that stare. 'I have to go now,' he said.

May glared crossly at him. 'I said you could stay, you silly! You don't want to go back.'

Tam smiled. It was good to be wanted, although

May was so strange. 'I'll come whenever I can,' he told her. He was thinking what a great thing it would be to pop over here for a few hours – to jump across for breakfast or for tea to play for a few hours. He'd have to think up some good lies for his mum, though – he'd already be in trouble for stopping so long. But May was all hunched up and angry.

'I can't run away from home,' he said, touching her arm.

'I would have,' said May, turning her little flat face to him. Tam saw that her eyes were wet and he was touched but he didn't understand. He'd only spent an hour or so with her. Then he realised; May was more than just funny. That flat note in her voice, her fears of going inside, even her pure affection for him. There was something not right with her mentally.

'I like you,' he said, touching her arm.

May suddenly put her arms around his neck and pressed her face very hard into his. He could feel her warm breath on his cheek. He held her stiffly. She was clumsy and pressed so hard it hurt his face. She meant it with all of her heart.

'Goodbye,' she said. She got up and ran away across the farmyard and disappeared around the side of the house. Tam watched her and waved but she didn't look back. All he had done was play with her and she adored him.

Winnie was following her but Tam grabbed her by the collar. It had been fun: now he had to get back.

'Where's Rosey, girl .... Rosey? Show me ...'

He wanted the dog and the old woman – just as it had been when he came, so he could get back.

Winnie seemed to understand. She walked towards the barn, looking back and wagging her tail. Tam followed. Now that it was time to go he was getting scared.

The old woman sat at the back of the barn away from the sun. She was hunched up in the shadows – so much like a shadow herself Tam would have missed her had Winnie not run up and licked her hand.

Tam stood and watched a moment. She lifted her hand to pet the dog as if she were lifting some great weight. Everything the beggar woman did was tired, old, dull – like the bees you sometimes found clinging to walls or leaves, who could no longer fly and moved their legs weakly.

Tam shuffled in the straw. 'So this is where you sleep ...' Tam said. She didn't seem to hear but her eyes moved. She was watching him.

Tam glanced anxiously back at the farmyard. He was frightened of her again. Although she seemed so useless she could move from world to world like a witch. She was mad and he relied on her to take him home.

He came closer. 'Thank you for taking me, Rosey – but I want to go home now,' he whispered.

Her lips moved in a tired echo of the word. 'Home ...' she mouthed.

'Yes, home ... you know ...'

The old woman stared at him. It was the first time he had seen her look so directly at anything. She made a gesture, as if there was something Tam could do. He stared back, not understanding, and suddenly she buried her face in her hands. She made no noise but held her face and began rocking to and fro, a pantomime of despair.

And yet when he took her arm her hands fell lifelessly down and her eyes were dry. Perhaps she had no tears. Her head hung. She had disappeared again.

Tam was frightened that he might be stuck here out of place, out of time. He wanted to shake her, to force her to take him home. But he remembered the dog and looked round for her. Winnie had gone.

'Winnie!' He was getting desperate. Grabbing Rosey's sleeve he pulled her across the yard to the place by the farmhouse where they had appeared. Perhaps Rosey could take him back on her own.

'Come on, Rosey, please take me home,' he begged. She did nothing. She was so useless, Tam could have hit her. He pushed her back into the wall, tried to press her back in time. But there was no sliding, no grey damp. The chickens clucked nearby, the sun glowed on the hill, going down now. A warm day in autumn. That still April day where his father waited for him was impossibly far away.

As Tam stood helplessly by the wall close to tears Mr Nutter walked around the corner carrying a bucket. He stopped dead when he saw him.

'Still here?' He looked at the wall, then at Tam's face. 'Art lost, lad?' he gave Tam a funny little smile. 'Mrs Wot's-'er-name'll be getting worried,' he said.

Rosey had begun to drift away back towards the barn. Tam took a couple of steps and grabbed her arm; he was frightened of losing her.

'Don't go,' he begged.

Rosey stopped. Tam looked back to Mr Nutter. The farmer was staring at him as if he were mad.

'It's all right, lad, it's all right,' he said.

Tam glanced at Rosey and back at the farmer. What was the matter, what had gone wrong suddenly? He saw Mr Nutter follow his glance, but his gaze wandered past he old woman, across the barn; then quickly back to Tam.

The farmer couldn't see Rosey.

He squeezed her arm to be sure she was there. He felt the skinny arm, was shocked at how little flesh there was on it. The old woman was looking round at him and she was as real as he was. Yet Mr Nutter couldn't see her, he was certain of it. His eyes were again searching for whatever it was that Tam held on to, spoke to, but he was missing her altogether.

Rosey was only here for Tam.

He began walking across the farmyard towards the gate. He was trying to keep his face still.

'No need to rush,' began Mr Nutter. But now the tears were here. It was impossible to explain, impossible to stay there, impossible to go ... Suddenly Tam was running. He heard Mr Nutter shout behind him. The farmyard flashed past. He saw Winnie watching him, May standing by the house with her mouth open and her arms open but it was too late. He couldn't answer any questions. He climbed the gate and ran up the hill. No one was following him. He glanced quickly back down at the farm before he dropped behind the ridge. Mr Nutter was at the gate staring after him. He shouted. May was behind him and when she saw Tam look she began to run towards him. But Tam turned and ran again down the hill towards the town. When he looked back, halfway over the dry stone wall between that field and the next, the farm was already out of sight.

Tam dropped over the wall and walked down to the town.

# Chapter 5

It was his town but it was another world. The houses were dark. The thin, spiralled metal chimney from the plastics factory was gone, but he could see ten or more brick stacks sticking up out of the town like blunt church spires, spilling dark smoke. There was smoke coming from many of the houses too. It sank down and smudged the valley. This other Cawldale lay under smoke, its people lived their lives in it. Below him, beyond the cricket pitch, beyond the allotments and fields, he could see his own house staring at him across the valley.

Tam glanced behind him. The farm was already out of sight.

The town became less and less familiar as he got closer. No TV aerials on the roofs, old crock cars and horses on the roads. The cricket clubhouse was gone, and there were more allotments over the river where new houses had stood. The council estate on the other side of the main road was no longer there and Tam could see a couple of strange buildings, churches or chapels, rising above the rooftops. The fields around him had more flowers, longer grass. Even the air was different; it tasted of soot.

And then Tam stopped and stared because there on the hillside was a team of horses ploughing. Two stubby, powerful horses with their manes flicking in the wind, their strong necks forward and fat leather halters around their shoulders. They toiled steadily around the hill with a man walking behind them, watching the plough share turn over the soil like a brown wave. A flock of crows followed them. The horses tossed their heads in the wind and pulled against the earth.

Tam felt like laughing again. He shook his head as if he could get rid of that image of the past and shake himself back to his own time, with big tractors and fields with short grass. But the horses strode around the hill, and the man held the plough handles with his strong arms and shouted at them; his voice came to Tam on the wind. He could even smell the horses. It was all real.

Tam knew where he was: Cawldale. But when? Mr Nutter had mentioned a war, but he had seen no signs of violence. First or Second? Suddenly Tam wasn't just afraid – he was curious. He ran on.

The bridge over the river was newer. Instead of tarmac there were stone slabs on it but underneath ducks still dabbed and quacked. They looked up at him out of one eye just as they used to – had, will – years later. They could have been the same ducks.

After the river, the allotments. Instead of the thick rows of willow trees that separated them from the path there was a fence of crooked wire running along with thin saplings planted at intervals.

Tam stood by the fence and looked in. The same rectangular garden plots laid neatly out, the same paths criss-crossing between them, the same vegetables in rows across the plots. But the greenhouses and tidy wooden sheds were replaced by little corrugated irons shacks leaning crookedly on the corner of every plot. Further on were the same houses and the same trees, their leaves and branches stirring in another wind.

A couple of men were talking some way off. They stood by the side of one of those tumbledown sheds, flat cloth caps on their heads and enormous trousers tied up round their waists. They had their sleeves rolled up. One wore an unbuttoned waistcoat. Tam watched as he pulled a pipe out of his mouth and examined the bowl. They stood differently – arms folded,heads up, all puffed up like prize horses. Now the man lifted up his foot and tapped the pipe out on the sole of his boot. Tam stared, goggle-eyed. His excitement fizzed on the edge of fear. That mad old woman had taken him right out of the world.

Another pair of men came walking along the path towards him. Tam stood awkwardly, waiting for them to pass. He tried to appear interested in the allotments but he cast a quick glance as they drew near. The men were staring at him.

'Hey, 'eck, what have we got here?'

'Looks like a bloody Martian.'

Of course, he thought – his clothes. Idiot! He made to run off but one of the men shot out a hand and grabbed him by the shoulder.

'Yowl wait till we're finished wi' you, my lad,' he said. Tam wrenched at his coat, tried to pull away, but to his astonishment the man gave him a powerful cuff round the ear.

'Hold still, will yer?' he demanded.

'Don't you hit me, you've no right to hit me,' cried Tam, struggling more violently than ever. No stranger had ever hit him. But the man only struck him again. Tam stopped struggling and stared at them. His eyes began to fill with tears, not because the blows hurt, although they did, but because it was humiliating to be hit by a stranger, and because he wasn't used to it.

'Don't be such a cry baby, it were nowt but a little tap,' said his attacker uncomfortably. Then he was cross again. 'Hold still or I'll give yer summat to cry about.'

'I'm not used to being hit, that's all,' said Tam, trying to keep his voice steady. 'Men don't hit women and children where I come from,' he added.

'Aye, well we do 'ere,' said the man; and gave him another cracking blow to the side of his head to prove it. 'Them as has no manners, anyhow,' he added.

But the other man seemed nervous and glanced up the road. 'Watch it wi' him, Jem,' he said. ''Appen he's some sort o' toff, the way he speaks.'

'Let you out wi'out yer nanny, have they?' demanded the first man. Tam waited for them to finish with him.

'Where does tha comes from?' asked the second man. He grabbed hold of Tam's anorak and fingered it. 'It feels like – I don't know what it feels like,' he added, glancing up at Jem, who also felt the material and shrugged.

Tam remembered what he had told the farmer. 'London,' he said. 'These are London clothes.'

'Like hell, they are. I've got southerners staying wi' us and they wear nowt like it,' said the second man.

'He's no toff, he don't talk like one and he don't act like one,' said Jem angrily. Both of them were staring down at him frowning. Tam saw anger, distrust – violence. He shrugged and tried to appear casual.

''Appen he's a spy,' said the second man suddenly. They both grinned.

'Aye – a German spy. What yer done wi' yer parachute?' asked Jem. They laughed. But it wasn't a pleasant laugh.

'You know what we do wi' spies here, don't yer?' asked the other. He seemed to have decided that Tam was nothing to fear. 'We shoot 'em. 'Appen we ought t' hand 'im over to Doddy, an' he can put him in nick till the army gets here to shoot him.'

Tam looked so terrified that the two men burst out laughing again.

'I'm not a spy – honestly,' he said.

'Boy spies – what'll Hitler get up to next?' demanded Jem. ''Ere – how long do you think you'll hold out under torture?' he asked, smirking at his mate.

'Interrogate 'im!'

'Aye! Now, you answer me, my lad – what'll I ask 'im, Harry?'

Harry had a think. 'Who's the Prime Minister of England?'

Tam knew the answer to that one. 'Mr Winnie,' he said promptly

But it was all wrong. The two men glanced at one another. Jem guffawed nervously. 'Everyone knows the answer to that,' he said. But the other man was looking curiously at Tam.

'He's a nutcase, that's what it is.'

''Appen?' demanded Jem, staring intently at Tam.

'Look at 'im – look at his face, he don't know what day it is. He's all – all wrong, int he?'

He was all wrong – wrong face, wrong voice, wrong clothes. He moved wrong, he thought wrong. Truly, Tam was lost in this other world.

Jem and Harry stared at him, their faces a mixture of curiosity, fear and disgust.

'Are you a nutter – I say, you're a nutcase, aren't you?' said the second man, shouting as if Tam would understand better that way.

'That's right,' agreed Tam. He let his head wobble just to prove it. The two men roared with laughter – proper laughter this time. They were relieved. They knew what he was.

Tam took his chance. He pulled suddenly away and bolted off down the path. Jem reached for him, but Tam shifted sideways and the man paused.

'Leave the beggar ...'

He ran fast past the cricket field, past a row of houses into the edge of town. He was near his own house now, but nowhere near home. There was an old garage on the corner – at least it had been a garage when he knew it. Now it seemed to be a farm building. A pair of big brown horses with white faces flashed past and a man glanced up as he ran. There were some children playing in the road before his house – not tarmac and paving now but just dirt, a dirt road in front of the house where he would live one day. The children stared at him, too. It must be his tell-tale clothes that gave him away. He didn't yet realise that he gave himself away just by being there.

Tam fled into the alley behind the row and dodged into a gateway. He had to get his breath back.

There was nowhere to hide. In front the houses stared in from both sides, separated from the road by only a strip of earth. At the back where Tam crouched, the alleyways were quieter and the houses were separated from the alleys by little paved yards. But each one of those yards was overlooked by a kitchen window and there was no way out of the alley but either end. If someone turned the corner Tam would stick out like a black beetle on a sheet of paper.

He had to change his clothes. He remembered what the kids he had just seen playing outside in the dirt had worn – suits of baggy trousers around their knees and jackets, some with waistcoats underneath. He hadn't given up the idea of exploring. He wanted to peer in at the windows of his house, go and see the shops in the main street, watch the people.

As soon as he got his breath Tam crept out of the gateway and made his way down the alley. In the yards and stretched across the alley every now and then, were washing lines. On one or two the washing was out.

He had to be quick. All they had to do was see him to know. Tam had spotted what he wanted – one of those suits and a grey shirt blowing in the wind – and he was peering round the gate to see if the way was clear when the cobbles clattered behind him. It sounded like a small herd of iron-shod horses. Tam winced and glanced back.

It was a gang of boys. They had just come out of one of the yards, strutting and slouching into the alley, hands in pockets or stuck under their braces. They were looking for fun – or trouble. They'd found it. The whole pack were goggling at him, from the big ones swaggering at the front to the little ones at the back sucking their fingers behind their big brothers – as if they'd just turned the corner and found a unicorn on the cobbles.

'Gerra load o' that,' said one.

The biggest of them pushed to the front, glanced from side to side at his mates, and began.

'Whatcha doin' on our patch?' he demanded, sticking his chin out at Tam.

'Just looking,' said Tam. He was already backing off.

At the sound of his voice the boys glanced at each other. Tam knew what that glance meant. He'd seen it a little while before between those two men. He fled.

The shout went up. The boys ran at him. Tam could hear them cracking and rattling in their clogs on the cobbles behind him.

Those boys were fierce and strong but they didn't stand a chance. Tam had fear jetting him off down the street. He lived in an age of better food and they were wary of his size and strangeness. Above all, they were running in wooden clogs, iron-shod, that struck fearsomely on the cobblestones, but slid and had no grip. Tam was in his trainers. By the time they had clacked and skidded their way halfway down the alley, Tam was off like a panther halfway along the next road. He could hear them shouting in surprise, already in the distance as he sped down another couple of roads to make sure. Then he stopped. There was a washing line in one of the yards ...

Tam crept back and peeped over the wall. It was

all there, baggy short trousers, jacket, even a waistcoat – the uniform of boys of this place. He checked the window to make sure everything was clear and then jumped into the yard to snatch it all off the line. Then, panic – people coming. Tam was trapped in the yard, right in front of the window. First it was a man coming home from work, kicking his clogs on the cobbles and whistling, his coat flung over his back. Then a young woman popped out to peg up a huge pair of white knickers and some vests on her line strung across the alley. Tam hid behind the shed, terrified. Now he was not only an alien, but a thief ... Next, a boy on a bike built like a tank with an enormous basket on the front with 'Soames Butchers' written in black letters on it. The bike rattled over the cobbles and round the corner. At last the way was clear.

Tam shot out of his hiding place, trailing his new clothes in his arms like a sparrow flying off with a beakful of hay. In the next street he found a big building, a Methodist Chapel. Tam jumped the wall and dropped down. He was in a tight gap between the wall and the building. No windows overlooked. He sighed and sank to the ground, exhausted with panic. For the first time since he'd come to Cawldale he was out of sight, out of trouble.

The sky was beginning to get dark. It wasn't just the sun going down. The chimney pots of the houses were coming to life – first one, then another, then another three suddenly belching thick smoke into the air. The smell of coal. As he'd dropped down behind the wall Tam had a glimpse of the sun over the hill above Thowt It – a low, red eye wreathed in dark colours and smoky haze. People were coming home from work and lighting their fires for cooking and hot water. Smoke was everywhere, you could see it blowing along in the wind, beating down on the roofs. Soon, Tam heard feet hurrying out and women chatting. They were taking their washing in before the smoke soiled it. Further off, in the next road, there was a fuss – shouting, people calling. One of the housewives had found her boy's clothes gone from the line.

Tam stayed where he was. He was losing his appetite for exploring. He listened to the people walking and talking – their voices, their ways, their thoughts all different from those he knew. He despaired of ever being able to hide among them, clothes or no clothes. He thought he might stay there hidden away till night came and then find a barn to sleep in, before getting back up to Thowt It in the morning. He had to get back home.

An hour went by. Tam got cold and bored. He began to hope that maybe his clothes would be enough disguise if he kept his mouth shut. He had an idea that there was something for him here after all: his house. There was no reason for it, but he felt it still belonged to him. If there was anyone to help him, it must be there.

He got out of his own clothes and wrapped them in his jeans, which he tucked under his arm. The little suit was too big, but half the kids in the street were in badly fitting clothes, so that didn't matter. They were damp, too, and he was already cold. The worst thing was that he had no braces and he had to keep his hands in his pockets to keep the trousers up. After some thought Tam decided to keep his trainers on. He couldn't go barefoot and even though it was more suspicious he could run in them. At least they were black and not the usual bright white kind. Even the grown men would have a job keeping up with him in clogs.

He slipped along the alley and out of the gate.

It was like something on TV. The clothes they wore, the things they did. A mother with a pram walked past, her hair bobbed around her shoulders. The pram was a huge thing, with enormous back wheels and a waterproof hood. You couldn't see the baby. She could have hidden her entire family in there. A girl standing in a front door stared curiously at him. Tam kept his head down and walked swiftly past two, three, four streets, until he was in Collard Road – his road.

Tam lived at number four. The house was much as he knew it – the same old-fashioned windows that his dad had refused to get rid of, the same front door. It had had hardboard over it when they'd moved in a few years ago but his dad had taken it off and now it was just the same as this. Only the colour was different. It was so much a part of his life that he felt he could go up and walk into normality. Whoever was in there would know, somehow ...

Outside in the dirt in front of his house a boy was playing with a couple of wooden cars. Tam walked slowly past, his hands deep in his pockets holding his trousers up. The windows to his house were shrouded in nets. There was a gap at the top but all he could see was a patch of ceiling and a cloth lampshade. The boy with the toy cars looked curiously up at him.

'Do you live there?' asked Tam, nodding at the house.

The child nodded sideways, still staring at him. 'That's our'n.' Next door – number six.

'But who lives at number four?' asked Tam. He looked up at the top windows. They stared back, revealing nothing.

'George an' Margaret,' replied the child. He forgot Tam and went back to his cars. Tam could hear him going 'brummm, brumm' under his breath.

Tam had never heard of George and Margaret. But he didn't give up hope. There must be some link with his world here, where he lived, someone else who had made the same journey as he had, perhaps ...

The front door at number six opened and a young woman looked out. 'Dennis – tea's ready. Hurry in and get yersel washed.'

Dennis, she had called the child. And in Tam's time Dennis lived there, still in the same house with his mam. Tam felt a surge of hope. That woman must be Dennis's mother, Eveline – kind Eveline, who always had a piece of fruit or cake or chocolate to give him – Eveline who would sit and chat all day and never throw him out. But it didn't look like her. Eveline was an old woman, bent, white, plump. This young woman had dark hair and was thin. She had rings under her eyes, she looked tired. But she was pretty and there was something about her – the way she moved her hands – that made him sure it really was Eveline. She held her arms out for Dennis to come to her and she looked at Tam. She smiled.

'Yer new here, aren't yer?' she asked him kindly.

Tam held out his hands. 'Eveline,' he said.

She shot him a glance. 'How d'yer know my name?' she demanded. 'Mrs Barker to you, my lad,' she added. She gestured impatiently at Dennis who was dawdling, staring again at Tam. Now he hurried up to her and she pushed him in behind her. She was frowning already as she looked to Tam. 'Not lost ... not lost, are you?' she asked uncertainly.

Tam nodded eagerly. She looked confused. He held out his arms again. He took a step towards her. 'Please Eveline don't you know me? It's me – it's Tam,' he said desperately.

Her face turned to anger. 'Don't you try your tricks wi' me. Go on, scarper ... we don't want your sort round here.' She flicked her dishcloth at him and Tam was certain it was her then because that movement was so typical of her when she shooed the cats off her little garden. But it was no use. She had nothing for him, she wanted to get rid of him. She shouted, 'Scram!' and slammed the door. For one second Tam considered going and knocking and begging her to take him in, because he was lost, really lost, more lost than anyone could be. But someone was rapping on the window, hard. Next door – his own house. A man was looking out. His mouth was open and his face was creased, ugly in anger. He was waving his hand at Tam.

'Go away ... go on ... go away!' he was shouting. Tam turned on his heels and walked as fast as he could down the road.

# Chapter 6

It wasn't just his clothes. He could never fool these people into thinking he was one of them. Even though they couldn't tell how and why or what it was, they knew he was wrong. He frightened them and they hated him for it; even Eveline, who was kind to all things, didn't trust him now.

Only Thowt It Farm was safe. He remembered what Mr Nutter had said. He could stay there if he liked. Mr Nutter was someone special. He knew Tam didn't fit, but he seemed to like him all the more for it.

Tam had walked away into the town and the streets were filling with people coming home from work. Tam could see them looking at him. The Methodist Chapel was nearby and he considered hiding there again until the streets were quiet. But he couldn't wait and turned round to walk back to the hill.

He was only one street away when the gang came back.

The first he knew of it was a rapid clatter on the cobbles and he looked back to see them flying towards him, a string of them down the road. Tam felt confident; he had his trainers. He jumped forward and sprinted down the alley. He was halfway down and leaving them standing when a couple of lads appeared in front of him.

'Gerrim, Jimmy, gerrim!' bawled the boys behind.

Tam swerved. Jimmy crouched low and made a dive for his legs and Tam skidded past him, but there was another boy still to pass. He swerved again but now his trainers, his magic shoes that carried him to safety, let him down. There was wet under him. He skidded as he turned and scraped the ground with his knees. He almost bounced off the stones and was up and running again but it was too late. The two boys jumped on him; he crashed to the ground. They climbed on him and sat there, one on his belly the other on his face. The others came from behind and dragged him to his feet.

'Yer for it now ...'

'Whatcha doin' on our patch? I'll show yer to come on our patch ...'

'What the 'ell is he?'

The boys were shoving at him. They didn't want any answers to their questions. Every time he tried to speak they shoved harder.

Tam began to fight back, looking for a gap to slip through. 'Leave me alone, leave me alone,' he was shouting. He tucked his head down and churned his arms, but fighting was their game. They shut up then and started on him hard, going for his face. He got a bloodied nose, his lip was knocked onto his teeth, then he was on the floor, hugging his precious parcel of clothes to him while those hard, iron-shod clogs were battering at him.

Tam rolled in a ball, groaning. They stood back to look down at their work.

'He speaks like a bloody Nancy!'

'... get back where you came from, Sissy ...'

'He's a German, that's what he is!'

'Thassit ...' they shrieked in delight. 'A spy, a bloody German spy!' None of them believed it, of course, but as with the men it seemed to explain something. They began to kick at him again, their voices shrill.

'Say summat in Kraut ...'

'Send this to 'itler ...'

Tam began to fear they would do him real damage. If they could, they'd have kicked him right out of their world.

But then a man's shout: heavy feet cracked on the cobbles. The boys shouted a name he'd heard before – 'Doddy!' – and they scattered like mice. Tam rolled over onto his side and covered his face.

'What you bin up to?' His arm was grabbed and he was hauled to his feet. A heavy blue uniform and a helmet – different from what he knew, but enough the same. A policeman. He peered at Tam's face angrily.

'They've done you over good and proper,' he muttered. He began dabbing at his cuts and wounds with a big white handkerchief.

'Evacuee?' he asked as he dabbed.

'Ouch, yes,' said Tam.

Doddy scowled. 'They should know better than to give strangers a battering, we're all in the same boat these days,' he growled. 'Who yer staying wi'?'

'Can't remember,' replied Tam.

The policeman gave him a funny look. 'You're a strong lad. You'll get over that battering. I'll give 'em hell when I catch 'em...' He shouted that, in case they were still nearby. 'But you're not right bright forgetting who yer staying wi',' he added.

'He's a bloody German spy, that's all!' shouted one of the kids from cover.

'Don't be daft, Billy Higgins, even 'itler don't have boy spies. And you aren't much brighter than he is … I'll know whose dad to have a word wi' now.'

No one replied. 'Billy's dad's a bit heavy wi' the buckle end of his belt,' grinned the policeman at Tam. Tam just groaned.

Doddy finished dabbing at the blood and stood back to give Tam a long careful look-over. 'You're a funny looking piece of work,' he said at last. There was a curious expression on his face. He felt sorry for Tam, he wanted to help him. But there was no mistaking that expression. The policeman already disliked him.

'I haven't done anything,' muttered Tam.

''Appen. Now then. What road you staying at?'

Furtively Tam glanced to one side down the road where he might run. But Doddy had a keen eye and he shot out a hand.

'Oh, no you don't.' He grabbed his arm and gave Tam a little shake. 'There's more to this than meets the eye, my lad.'

Tam began to pull away. 'I haven't done anything …' he complained. But Doddy had a good grip on him. He gave Tam another shake – a hard one this time – and Tam's bundle fell from his arms. His jeans, sweatshirt and anorak fell out on the cobbles.

'Now …' The policeman bent and picked them up. 'This is a bit nice – too good fer the likes o' you. I've not seen the like of this before,' he muttered suspiciously, fingering the strange material with one hand and holding onto Tam's arm with the other.

'They're mine,' said Tam sullenly.

The policeman snorted with derision. 'Oh, aye. Now, what are you up to ... 'ere ... these are all damp ...' He was feeling the stolen shirt on Tam's arm. And now he knew. 'You pinched these, didn't you? Pinched 'em off Mrs Shuttleworth's line. She told me her lad's clothes had been nicked. You bloody little thief. We don't like thieves round here.' He gave Tam another hard shake. His face had gone cold. 'I knew there was summat about you an' now I know what ... a little thief, come up from South to help yerself. There's a few more things to find out about you, I reckon. I think we'd better put you somewhere nice and safe while I make a few enquiries.' The policeman began to pull Tam up the road.

Behind them the streets echoed: 'Thief! Thief!' The gang was still watching. They'd heard it all.

'You lot run along – I'll take care of this 'un.'

'We'll 'ave 'im ...' one of them shouted back. Tam heard them run off out of sight, like birds flying in the night.

The policeman marched Tam down the dark, smoky roads, his hand locked firmly around his arm. Tam was sick. What would happen when they investigated and found that he came from nowhere? Would they really think he was a spy? Such things happened in wartime. But he was just a boy, they didn't shoot boys, surely ... Even if they didn't he had a story no one would believe. Once he was locked up he would never get away, trapped in this world where he wasn't normal any more.

Although he wasn't fast or bold, Tam knew that he had to escape. He pretended to trip. He flung himself sideways and twisted round and round to make the policeman lose his grip. But Doddy merely reached down the other hand to his collar and pulled Tam right off his feet into the air.

'I'm wise to all them tricks,' he said grimly and dealt Tam a hard, rapid series of blows on his ears. 'Don't try owt again.' He set off, his grip harder than ever on Tam's upper arm, wrenched high up so that Tam had to walk half on tiptoes. It was impossible to try anything.

Night was closing in. People had finished their evening meal, and they found time to peer curiously out of windows or pause in the streets to watch the policeman march the boy with the odd haircut and baggy trousers down the road.

'What you got there, Doddy?' called a man in shirt sleeves and braces from his doorway.

'Nasty little thief. Pinching clothes off washing lines.'

'You get a lot o' dirt flung up in a war ...'

Now they turned off the big road to cut through a warren of small, old houses that had gone in Tam's time. These little streets smelt of chickens, kept in coops in the back yards and fed on scraps, of damp and soot and boiled potatoes. After a few minutes they came out on the edge of a bigger road. A car was coming past, puttering and chugging, an old van with flaky paint and wheels with spokes. The policeman paused on the edge of the dark street while it went past.

They were halfway across the road when Tam had the impression of a small patch of darkness moving rapidly towards them. Then there was a hard thud. The policeman's breath wheezed out of him, he doubled up and fell to the ground. Something was attacking him, something ferocious that raged and snarled. Doddy lay on his back, desperately fending it off with his feet. Tam stepped back. The animal, whatever it was, looked surprisingly small for something making so much noise. Then May was pulling his hand.

She said something, but she was so excited she only made a flat honking. They ran together back into the damp warren behind them. For another second they heard Winnie still raging and worrying the fallen policeman. Then, silence and she was wagging her tail by their side and asking to be congratulated. There was no time.

'It's that bloody lunatic from Nutter's ...' Doddy was back on his feet and giving chase.

May knew those narrow streets well. She dodged and swerved, and Doddy's steps faltered behind them. They came to a yard lined with derelict sheds and workshops. May dragged him in and began clambering over a heap of rubbish lying against one of the walls. It was ridiculous, it just led to a steep wall they couldn't climb and the policeman was fast behind them. But hidden at the top under some old boxes was a narrow opening. May dropped out of sight as if she was falling through the rubbish. Tam almost fell in after her into a small room. Then Winnie came through, wriggling through the narrow window like a fat mouse and dropping on top of him into the darkness just in time. Doddy ran past. He paused at the yard, ran further up the road, then came back and began checking the shed doors and kicking at the cardboard boxes. Tam bit his lip but May sat calm and still, holding his arm. It seemed obvious where they were. But the policeman didn't know about the hidden door and in a minute he left.

In the quiet that followed Tam heard his own ragged breath. He wasn't just out of breath; he was terrified. He couldn't speak. May groped for his hand and held it to her face.

'I've got you back,' she said. 'I knew you were lost, like me. It's dangerous to go into the town during the day. I only ever go in the night. Thowt It Farm is the only safe place. I told you to live with us. You can't get lost on the farm.'

She seemed to know what he'd been through. He had a wild, hopeful idea. 'Do you ... do you come from the 1990s as well?' he asked her.

May frowned. She didn't know what he meant. 'You're like me,' she insisted. 'I never met anyone lost like me. Winnie found me,' she said proudly, patting the dog's head. 'She helped find you, too.'

Tam didn't want to be like her. 'It's not that ... I'm just in the wrong place,' he tried to explain.

May nodded. She understood perfectly. 'Yes, I know,' she told him. 'But I've found you again.' And she smiled to herself, full of pride.

Tam gave up trying to explain. He nodded. 'You found me,' he agreed.

'And now we're together again,' said May.

'Can we go back?' he asked. May pointed up to the

skylight. A little pale light still shone through. 'When the middle of the night comes.' She folded her arms around her legs. They had to wait.

Outside, the voices of the strange world. Men and women and children walked past chatting in a thick accent, like the one Tam knew but so strong he could often not understand what they were saying. Like, but different ... And so it was with everything – the smells of damp wood and stone and rotten food from the shed where he hid, the coal smoke in the air, the smells of cooking that wafted past from time to time – everything was familiar but twisted out of shape, just as he was to these people.

As the night advanced it got colder. Tam's clothes were damp and he was soon frozen through. May climbed up and dug about in the rubbish until she found some newspapers and cardboard. She showed him how to wrap it round himself. Now there were few people out – just the occasional man's voice.

'The pub,' explained May. Outside it was pitch black but she still wouldn't go. 'The middle of the night,' she insisted. 'I never go out else ... there's that policeman still about and lots of people.'

Together they made a little nest. She curled up on one side and got Winnie on the other side. She squeezed up against him and gradually the warmth began to creep into Tam's cold limbs and into his bones. Everything became soft and comfortable, as if those old newspapers were fluffy duvets. Tam gave May a squeeze.

'You rescued me,' he told her drowsily. 'I'd never have escaped ...'

'I knew you were like me when I saw you right at the beginning,' said May.

Is that what it's like for her? thought Tam. And then fell asleep.

The darkness was so deep and perfect and still that nothing changed when he opened his eyes. Only right next to him was the sound of the newspapers rustling. May touched him. Tam felt like a mouse awakening in the night under the boards in a great, still, sleeping house.

She said nothing but he knew it was time to be moving. May climbed up to the window. Tam handed up Winnie, then climbed up himself. They rolled down the heap of rubbish, crept across the yard and paused, waiting to be sure no one had heard them disturb the night. Then they stole out onto the streets.

With the night, all signs that this was the world he knew had vanished. There were no windows still lit at this hour, no moon, no street lights in that wartime world. Everything was shadows and shades of darkness and quietness everywhere. Only their own breath and footsteps moved and the faint light of a few stars was pale on the walls and cobbles of the road.

May led him home secretly through the streets. She was careful and cunning, checking to make sure each road was clear; she was an alien too. Winnie kept protectively close by her side, sometimes running ahead, sometimes lingering to sniff at a wall or a lamppost but never far away.

At last they were crossing the bridge at the edge of

town, the houses all behind them. Tam could make out the dark beast's back of the hill above. Already, Cawldale had all but vanished behind them into the darkness. As they were crossing the first field the town began to cry out. It moaned. The moan rose to a howl. Tam froze and crouched in the grass, shivering. The cry continued, rising and falling from moan to howl in a slow, regular pulse.

May touched his arm. 'Air raid,' she said softly. Through his fear he recognised it; it was a siren. He had heard them on films. This was war; the German planes were coming.

Tam thought ... bombs.

He turned to look down on the little town. Blackout. Tam had heard the word before but now he knew what it meant. Every light had to be hidden, every house had to become dark so that the little town could hide from the planes, tucked away in the black hillsides. A place the size of Cawldale could become invisible in the night.

A little further on he had another fright. Ahead, something was rising – a bright line up into the sky. Then there was another, then another. One by one a series of long, white antennae lifting up, up, up until they felt the clouds, like the long stiff feelers of some enormous insect hidden behind the hill. In his nervous state Tam stared, appalled for a second before he knew what they were – searchlights. Above him the bombers were flying. These powerful lights casting bright patches on the clouds were searching for the German planes. Tonight, people would die – those men in the planes thousands of metres above the earth, families like his own huddled down in the hidden town, wondering where the bombs would land.

'They never bomb Cawldale,' said May. 'They're going on to Manchester or Blackburn. But they'll go into their shelters anyway. It's all a big game.' Tam could hear Mr Nutter in her voice – it was just the sort of thing he would say.

As he crawled up the hill Tam kept his eye on the beams of light in the hope he might see a plane trapped like a moth in the beam, but there was nothing. As suddenly as they appeared, the lights went out. Tam stopped in his tracks, because now they really were in total darkness. But May gripped his hand and seemed quite at ease. She walked calmly across the pitted meadow and laughed at him, floundering and falling over every tussock. Shortly afterwards the all-clear sounded, a long steady wail out of the darkness and Tam's nerves were so shattered that he flung himself back down again, even though he had been waiting for it.

Down in its secret valley, Thowt It was not as well hidden as the town. The farmyard light was still on. From the air, the farm must be the only place visible for miles.

'Mr Nutter won't turn it off,' explained May.

Something big ran at the gate as they drew near. It hit the gate violently and there was an explosion of barking. Winnie ran forwards and uttered a low growl. From behind the gate came a little whine.

'Winnie's in charge, they all do what she tells them,' said May proudly.

In the farmhouse a window opened and Mr Nutter's voice floated out across the dark hills.

'Shut that racket!'

The dogs began to amble back from the gate. May climbed over into the farmyard.

'You can stay with me,' she said. Tam followed her but she didn't take him up to the house. Instead she stopped at her favourite spot – Winnie's dog kennel.

She turned to smile encouragingly at Tam before dropping to her knees and crawling inside. Her head appeared a second later. 'Come on, then,' she said. Tam had never known of anyone sleep in a dog kennel before, but this one was no ordinary kennel. It was lined with eiderdowns, above and below and all around. It was May's bedroom. The kennel was much too big for just Winnie.

'Mr Nutter made it for me,' boasted May. The two children beat around at the fleecy, fluffy down to make a deep nest for themselves. Then Winnie came in, walking on everyone and wagging her tail and licking faces.

They fought her off before they got too wet. ' Mr Nutter says it saves washing me,' giggled May. Then, like a little cat, she curled up in a ball. Tam lay back. It was so snug and warm he had to poke his toes out to keep cool. Winnie lay on top of them both.

Tam closed his eyes. He was tired ... so tired that he could feel himself melting, his bones floating away ...

'You were lost – out there on your own ...' said May sadly.

'Really lost,' said Tam. 'You rescued me,' he added, 'you and Winnie.'

Now that he was safe again he felt suddenly grateful and close to her. He really was lost, out of time, out of place – just like her. Until she had found him.

Even in the darkness he could feel the intensity of her look – one of those piercing clear looks that seemed to strip you to nothing.

'I was lost once,' she said. 'Mr Nutter found me.' She sighed.

He could feel her watching him as he fell asleep.

## Chapter 7

May wrapped him in a ball of eiderdowns like a skinny little nestling, deep in down, and he knew nothing of his troubles that night. The next thing, someone was shaking him awake and washing his face at the same time.

For a second he was confused, then thrilled as he found himself lying with his feet in the early morning mist and his face being licked by a dog. And then his spirits sank suddenly and without warning as he remembered: he was lost.

'Wake up – it's milking,' urged May in her strange, fluting voice. Tam stretched and groaned. He ached from head to foot. His nose was throbbing and his lip had puffed up and there were scabs on his knees where he had fallen. When he put his head out of the kennel it was like plunging it into cool, soft water. It was very early morning. The dew lay silvery like the surface of a lake over the hills. The smell of cows, someone clanking a bucket nearby. Then a cow lowed.

'Milking,' insisted May. Tam crawled right out and looked behind the kennel. One by one, a long line of cows were strolling through the farmyard and into the milking shed. Tam wrapped an eiderdown around his shoulders and followed with May after them.

Each cow knew her stall and walked quietly to her place and waited. Mr Nutter was already milking, squatted on a stool with his head pressed into the flank of a big brown cow. Tam could hear the milk jetting and ringing in the bucket underneath.

'That's Dandelion,' whispered May. 'She always gets in first.' She pointed out the cows one by one: 'Blossom, Daisy, Marigold, Early Purple ...'

'That's a funny name,' whispered Tam back.

'Early Purple Orchid. It's a flower that grows round here, he calls them all after the flowers,' explained May. She pointed to another cow just moving to stand quietly in her stall, waiting her turn. 'We called her Turnip, because she kept escaping into the turnip field.'

They laughed. Mr Nutter looked up. Framed in the doorway, May was holding an apparition wrapped in an eiderdown by the hand. It was a good five or six seconds before he recognised Tam.

'Ey, thump,' he said. 'What happened to you?'

Tam had no idea how he looked. His head stuck out of the eiderdown like something from the ghost train. He had dried blood all over his face, his puffed-out lip was the colour of plums, one eye was half closed and sticking together,.

'Mrs What's-her-name said I could stay. May put me up in the kennel,' lied Tam hopefully.

Mr Nutter's eyebrows ascended. 'What did you say Mrs Wot's-'er-name's name was?' he demanded.

'Oh ...'

'You must remember by now.'

'Mrs, er ... something beginning with H ...' said Tam at random.

'Higginbottom?'

'That's her,' he said gratefully.

'Her at the bottom o' Cowgill?' demanded Mr Nutter.

'Yes ...'

'Oh, well, I'll drop round later and give her my best.'

Tam's face fell.

'Don't worry,' said Mr Nutter. 'Mrs Higginbottom and I haven't spoken a word for twenty year or more. Not surprising,' he added, 'seeing as how she doesn't happen to exist. Now then ...' Before Tam could reply he got up and carried the milk bucket over to them. May crept round behind Tam as he got close.

Mr Nutter put the half-full bucket of warm milk by Tam's feet and dropped a ladle in it. 'Drink tha fill ... Mrs Pickles won't be here for a couple of hour to make us breakfast. 'Appen May'll take you up to house for a wash and brush up and get some clothes on you.' When he said her name the girl looked quickly at him – suspiciously, nervously – and then away. She didn't answer.

'Tha friend's cold, May,' said Mr Nutter. 'Wilt take him up after and find summat fer him to wear?' May glanced towards the house anxiously. Then she nodded quickly. She looked up to the beams of the old shed and said, as if to herself, 'He lives here, now.'

Mr Nutter gazed at her. ''Appen,' he said. He watched her as she squatted down to begin on the milk before going back to his cow.

The milk was warm and rich and tasted of cows more than ever. Tam didn't care, he loved it now. He let it fall down his throat in great long gulps. He hadn't eaten a thing since the bacon and eggs the day before. Mr Nutter watched from his milking stool.

'Ey, lad,' he said at last. 'Had trouble in town?'

Tam nodded.

'Lads?'

'Yes.'

Mr Nutter nodded. 'They're a rough lot. Not bad-hearted – they've good hearts every one of them, once they take to you. But there's something about thee, Tam. I can't put me finger on it ...'

'I don't know what it is,' said Tam in a high voice. 'It wasn't like this before ...'

Mr Nutter shook his head. 'It's the same wi' our May, int it, May?'

And the child shot him an intense glance from under her eyebrows, as if she could see right through him.

'Tha friend's in same boat, May love, but you know your way about better. Tek care of him, won't yer?'

She gave another quick nod, looking elsewhere as if it were only to herself.

Mr Nutter went back to milking the cow. His eyes had gone red again.

'Don't mind me,' said Mr Nutter, when he saw Tam looking. 'I'm always at it.'

When the ladle couldn't pick up any more, May tipped the bucket over so that Winnie could lap up what was left. Then she took Tam by the hand and led him across the farmyard to the house. Winnie followed, but lay down at the door.

'She's not allowed in the house, except the kitchen sometimes,' explained May. She looked nervously up at the house before she pushed the door open and tiptoed in.

May stole down the hall and up the stairs as if she were a thief expecting the real owners to come home at any moment. She led Tam to an enormous chest of drawers on the landing. Tam had to help her pull open the deep bottom drawer.

'Go on, then,' said May, looking warily towards the stairs. You'd think they were raiding the safe.

Tam poked about. It was mainly girls' clothes. He didn't fancy wearing a dress.

'I wear boys' clothes, sometimes,' said May. She began riffling through the drawer impatiently. To Tam's horror she was flinging clothes all over the floor.

'Hey...!' he exclaimed, but she frowned and snapped, 'It doesn't matter.'

The drawer was half empty before she found what she was looking for – a pair of overalls Tam's size, a jumper, a thick cotton shirt.

'You can have them if you like,' she said.

She began tugging at him at once to leave.

'But what about all these?' asked Tam pointing at the mess of clothes deep on the floor. 'We should put them back.'

'No, no ... come on ...' She carried on pulling at him and she seemed to be getting upset.

'I have to get washed,' he reminded her.

May groaned. 'In the kitchen,' she said. She almost fled down the stairs. Tam followed her down, and she pointed to the kitchen. 'I'll wait outside for you,' she yelped, and ran out of the door.

Tam shrugged and got on with his washing. He got

a good look at his face. He'd taken a proper bashing; those lads had wanted to hurt him. Washing wasn't easy. He had a sore nose, a sore lip, a sore eye – just to touch it made him wince. All he could do was soak and dab at it. But he got off the worst of it anyway. Then he got out of his old clothes and into the ones May had found for him. The shirt was a bit small but the overalls were just right. Tam looked like a regular farmer, now. He dressed quickly, keen to be back to the cows. Now that he was at Thowt It, life was interesting again. He wanted to milk a cow, he wanted to make butter. He could almost forget that he was lost.

May was waiting on the doorstep with Winnie and they ran back to the milking parlour together. Tam tried to explain to Mr Nutter about the mess but he just waved his hand. 'Mrs Pickles'll see to it ...'

May grabbed a little stool and a bucket as soon as she got in. 'I'll show you ...' She ran up to a cow and sat herself down by the beast's side with the bucket in position and tucked her hands under her armpits – 'To warm them up for Blossom,' she explained, before she got to milking. Winnie followed her and lay down at her side as she tried to show Tam what to do.

It took Tam ages to get the knack. First the milk wouldn't come out, then it dribbled, then it squirted all over the place, then he squeezed too hard and the cow kicked the bucket over. He glanced enviously at May, who was an expert. At one point he noticed her squirting little jets of milk in the air for Winnie to jump up and catch in her mouth. Mr Nutter saw it too.

'That's enough o' that,' he growled. 'Dog's gettin' fat.'

At last Tam found how to squeeze the milk out in fierce little jets that hissed and rang in the metal pail. But he was still slow. He'd only milked one cow by the time they were done. May had done three in that time and Mr Nutter at least ten.

Mr Nutter poured the last bucketful into the big vat to one side of the shed. He straightened up and held his back. 'Getting older faster,' he complained. Meanwhile, May had crept to the back of the shed. He gave her a nod. 'Go on, then May – do yer stuff!'

'Yowp, yowp, yowp!' cried May. The cows started in their stalls and began backing out. Winnie barked, wagging her tail excitedly. The cows began banging out of their stalls and the quiet, misty atmosphere of morning milking was broken to pieces. May was running up and down the stalls like a quick little dog, herding the cows out into the yard. She and Winnie worked as a team, she going round one side, the dog on the other, running up close to the heels of any animal that tried to stray.

Two other dogs appeared warily waving their tails. They looked guiltily up at Mr Nutter but he hushed them and told them to lie.

'Done you out of a job, she has,' he remarked, patting their heads and ruffling their ears. 'Poor old things. Now you know what it is to get the sack. Ah, well, but she's better at it. Ey, May, which field today?' he shouted.

'Moorside!' she called back.

'Good girl, off you go. You can help her while I get on wi' mucking out,' said Mr Nutter to Tam. 'Then it'll be time fer us breakfast, and you can meet our Mrs Pickles. And we'll see what she has to say.'

'Come on, come on,' called May. Tam ran after her. Once out of the farm gate the cows seemed to know the way, and he and May followed behind with Winnie just jumping forward to snap at a slowcoach if she stopped to eat the grass by the hedgerow for too long.

As they walked, Tam quizzed May. No, she wasn't Mr Nutter's daughter or grand-daughter. Her parents were dead. She'd been living with him for a few years. When he asked her where she had lived before she frowned.

'I was lost ... like you,' was all she would say.

Questions made May uncomfortable, so instead he talked about Mr Nutter and the farm and how it worked and what they did. And May chatted away twenty to the dozen on that subject; she loved the farm. There and only there, she was at home. She was ill at ease with the rest of the world – like him. But she didn't come from another world or time. She was bright and quick, although there seemed to be something missing. Tam wondered what could have made her so strange and fearful.

The sun was coming up and warming away the morning mist. May had been working hard and now she rolled up the sleeves of her thick cotton shirt. Tam saw with shock that her arm had been broken at some time and very badly set – there was a noticeable lump where the bones had knitted together and the arm turned inwards, like a crab's.

'What happened to your arm?' he asked.

'Broke it,' said May shortly. She said nothing more, but he noticed that she rolled her sleeve down again a few minutes later.

As they got near the house the farmyard smells of cows and muck and straw and chicken mingled with another smell – bacon frying. Tam's mouth flooded. In the window, with her arms in the sink, he could see a thin, red-faced woman. She scowled and went into the room when she saw them.

'Mrs Pickles. Always cross,' said May. She began to wander off towards the barn. Tam stared after her.

Beyond, standing in the dark of the barn by the stacked hay, old Rosey stood. Her bundled clothes made her look like a stack of hay herself in the dim light, but it was her all right and she was watching him. But then her head dropped, her gaze slipped away to whatever unhappy thoughts she lived with. Tam felt a pang of fear. He had forgotten for a while, talking to May, helping on the farm. But suddenly he wanted very badly to be home.

Tam went to go to her but Mr Nutter appeared at the farmhouse door and waved him to come in.

'This is our Mrs Pickles, as does us cleaning and cooking,' he said.

Mrs Pickles stood on the kitchen flags drying her hands on her pinny and inspected him closely. 'Always cross,' May had said. Right now she was scowling.

'Bin in trouble,' she said at last, nodding at Tam's beaten face.

''Appen,' said Mr Nutter.

She shot out a thin hand and gripped Tam by the

hand and gave him a good shake. 'How d'ye do, Tam?' she shouted it at him, as if he were deaf or something. Tam backed off.

'Very well, thank you,' he said.

'Flesh and blood, same as me and you,' she told Mr Nutter triumphantly, as if that proved anything. 'A boy.'

''Appen,' said Mr Nutter.

Mrs Pickles stared him up and down a moment longer. Then – 'He's not right,' she declared.

''Appe ...' began Mr Nutter. But she rounded on him.

''Appen!' she said scornfully. ''Appen doesn't tell us where he came from, or who he is, or what he's doing here. 'Appen doesn't say why he looks so – so misbegotten, does it? Excuse me, lad,' she said, raising her voice to Tam. Mrs Pickles always remembered her manners, even when she was being cross. But Tam couldn't understand why she was so loud.

'God knows who he is and where he comes from and that's good enough f'me,' declared Mr Nutter.

Mrs Pickles turned away and shook the frying pan, which was sizzling on the stove under a thick layer of bacon. She tutted loudly. Mr Nutter winked at Tam and nodded up at the old one-handed clock. 'That old clock's gone off its head again,' he teased.

'It's another mouth to feed, Sam Nutter, that's what it is.' She turned to Tam. 'Don't get me wrong, boy,' she said, yelling again, '... you may be all right and you may be all wrong, time will tell. But it's another mouth to feed and Mr Nutter has enough on his plate, what with her out there ...'

'She likes him. You saw 'em come in the gate together.' Mr Nutter spoke of this as an impressive achievement, but Mrs Pickles was determined not to be impressed.

'But what does he think of her?' demanded Mrs Pickles. 'But what do you think of her?' she bellowed at Tam.

Tam said, 'She's my friend.'

Mrs Pickles looked surprised and shook the frying pan vigorously. 'It's the first I've heard that said,' she admitted grudgingly. 'Mind, it takes one to know one. You'll have to get him notified at Town Hall and all. Ten to one he's on the run from something or someone,' she added, casting a suspicious glance at Tam.

Mr Nutter shook his head. 'It's nowt to me what he is out there,' he said, jabbing his big flat head sideways at the world in general. 'He's an angel for my May, that's all I know.'

Mrs Pickles began tutting again. 'If all you have to do to be an angel is lose your wits I'll stop going to Church and start banging my head against a brick wall.' She glared at Tam. 'They didn't treat you like an angel down in Cawldale by all accounts,' she bawled.

'Why is she shouting at me?' asked Tam.

'Because she thinks you're a nutcase,' replied Mr Nutter promptly. Mrs Pickles rattled the frying pan nervously. Tam blushed.

'No, I'm not ... I just ... I'm just in the wrong place, that's all,' he finished lamely.

'Aye, and so are a good many more than admits to it,' declared Mr Nutter.

'I don't hold it against you, Tam,' said Mrs Pickles more quietly. But she soon forgot and began yelling at him again. She did it to May, too.

'What you need, Sam Nutter, is someone to look after you ... not more to look after,' she said at last in a softer voice. 'There's not many as'd be willing to help with two such as these ...'

Mr Nutter winked at Tam and said in a loud whisper, 'Mrs Pickles thinks as I should marry again ... and she thinks as it's Mrs Pickles I should be marrying.'

Mrs Pickles did not contradict him, but she blushed a deep and wonderful red, just like a tomato, and ordered Tam to the sink to wash for breakfast. By the time he'd done the table was decked with a clean blue and white cloth and set with four places, plates, side plates, cups and saucers and everything like a posh tea shop, with a big serving dish piled up with mushrooms, sausages, bacon, eggs and fried bread.

'May! Grub!' bellowed Mr Nutter from the door. He paused and shouted as an afterthought, 'Whyn't you come and have breakfast wi' us today – tha friend don't like eating on his own.' Mrs Pickles snorted derisively. But a couple of minutes later when they were all sitting around and Mrs Pickles was serving out the food, May crept in and sat herself inconspicuously at the chair nearest the door. Mrs Pickles goggled.

'I never thought I'd see that child sit down wi'out being tied to it,' she mumbled.

Mr Nutter beamed. 'Now, Susan, we'll say grace if you're ready.'

Tam folded his hands and looked at May. She already had her fork in one hand but she wasn't using it. She was shovelling the food into her mouth with the other in a large, scooping motion. Winnie was sitting bolt upright by her side nodding her head rapidly – yes, yes, yes, yes, begging for food, and May was feeding her bits of egg out of her fingers. Then she noticed the spare sausages on the serving plate and began pinching them even before she'd finished her own. Tam was goggling at her holding a sausage in the air with her fingers while she licked the fat off the end when Mrs Pickles gave a cough.

'It's rude to stare,' she pointed out.

'Sorry,' muttered Tam. Both Mr Nutter and Mrs Pickles, who was obviously a bit of a one for manners, sat there politely ignoring everything as if May were the Queen of England. But then she knocked over her cup of tea with her elbow and Mrs Pickles could stand it no longer. She turned bright red, glared indignantly and began tutting desperately.

'I swear that old clock needs seeing to, it'll tick itself off wall at this rate,' remarked Mr Nutter. Mrs Pickles shut up. Grace was said over the rattle and slurp of May's breakfast.

Mr Nutter said grace in a loud voice, rather as Mrs Pickles spoke to Tam – as if God were a bit deaf and none too bright. He kept glancing up at the ceiling as if He were sitting in their attic with His ear to the floor, listening in.

'Well, it's been a grand day so far,' he began. Mrs Pickles began tutting right away but he silenced her with a lifted finger. 'Cows have performed well, weather's looking right for the time o' year. Most of all we've got our May in kitchen to eat wi' us for the first time – we've got all that to thank You for. And there's Tam. It were a grand thought to send the boy as a friend fer May. I just hope You're not mucking him around too much in the doing of it.'

Mrs Pickles had begun to bristle and tut again. Mr Nutter went on loudly, 'As fer those You've seen fit not to show what You're up to – well, I can understand their doubts so I'm sure You can. After all, there's plenty none of us can understand, isn't there? Folk flying in the sky dropping fire on each other and the like, hundreds and thousands dying. I just hope You know what You're up to, that's all.'

'What a note to end grace on!' exclaimed Mrs Pickles, unable to restrain herself any longer. 'And in front of children, too! Grace should be an occasion of thanksgiving.'

'God gets thanked quite enough in my opinion,' replied Mr Nutter. 'I expect He appreciates a bit o' straight talking once in a while.' He explained to Tam, 'Mrs Pickles thinks I'm a bit too familiar wi' the Old 'Un. But what I say is – He made me like I am, so He'll just have to put up wi' me, won't He?'

Mrs Pickles snorted. 'In your opinion!' she scoffed. And she said a little prayer of her own to excuse the farmer before she began to eat.

May didn't stay at table long. By the time Tam was just beginning she'd scoffed all hers plus most of the seconds. Then she was sliding sideways off her chair, glancing anxiously at Mr Nutter and Mrs Pickles who pretended not to notice.

'See you after,' she hissed at Tam. She sank to the

floor and slid off on her hands and knees as if she could be neither seen nor heard.

'Well!' exclaimed Mrs Pickles. 'I never did!'

'Told yer,' beamed Mr Nutter. He smiled proudly at Tam, as if it were all his doing.

After breakfast, Mr Nutter got up and took some photographs from the dresser.

'I want to introduce you to my family, Tam,' he said. He showed him a picture of a stout lady in a pinny. 'My Martha ... my missus as was.' He stared at the lost face for a moment and once again his eyes misted over.

Mrs Pickles coughed irritably. Nr Nutter blew his nose and apologised and turned to the second photo.

'Our Ali,' he said proudly.

The photo showed a young woman in uniform. She was sitting on a swing with her legs prettily crossed, smiling at the camera. 'Our only child. We'd a liked more but Ali's made up for the ones we never had. She's abroad at the moment. Army. Bloody war. She's a lovely girl. I hope you'll meet her one day, Tam.'

Mr Nutter put the photograph on the table. 'Now I'll tell you a little story about our Ali and you'll understand the sort of girl she is and a bit more about all of us here.

'It were about four year back,' he began. ' I were working in cowshed when there's a car in our yard; our Ali – unexpected like. There were a young man wi' her. I knew summat were up, because she'd no leave due and you can't just go off where you will in the army.

'"What's up, Ali?" says I – thinking this were her young man and she were getting married, I were.

'"Dad," says she – and she gives me a long look, so's I know I'm on the line – "Dad, there's so much love going to waste up here since Mum died – do you think you could spare a bit of it for a poor orphan girl?"

'Well, I were flattered; and I'd bin thinking about taking in some evacuees. "'Appen," I says.

'"Right," says she. "Come wi' me."

'Well, you can't just up and off from a farm, no more than you can in the army. But that's what young man were for – to take care o' farm while I were off. So I changes me clothes, hops into car. And off we go.'

Mr Nutter gazed over Tam's head as he recalled that day. 'Seems there'd been a stick o' bombs fallen on a terrace nearby where Ali were stationed. Knocked the whole row flat. Well, they had their lists of who lived there. Went and dug 'em out, mostly dead. Roped the area off and that was that – or so they thought.

'Trouble was, stories started up. Folk saying they could hear noises – a child crying at night, tapping noises, screams even. No one took much notice at first. Seems there's often such stories around bombed houses. All the tales were around this one house where an old man and his daughter had lived. Daughter was a bit retarded, old man kept hisself to hisself. They'd both been killed. No children. Folks were hearing a child where no child had lived. But the stories didn't go away. Days passed. A week. More and more reports, more and more worried people. So they dug down. Got right down to basement before they found her. All alone under all that rubble. Four-year-old girl.' Mr Nutter shook his head. 'What it must have been like for her down there. A whole week ...'

'But where did she come from?' asked Tam.

'No one knows for sure. The theory they came up wi' is that she were the daughter o' that retarded girl by her own father. It happens. And they'd to hide her, you see. Hidden her away, never to come out in the air, never to see the light, never to know the sun or the grass. That cellar were her whole world: one dark room. Hidden away to hide their shame, though it were nowt to do wi' her. Maybe. One thing's for sure – she weren't right well treated before they found her. She had wounds, broken bones from way back.

'"Thing is, Dad – you'll see how it is wi' her," says Ali. "She won't talk to folk, just sits there all day locked up in herself – never moves an inch from dawn to dusk. You'll think she's blind, deaf and dumb, and yet there's nowt wrong wi' her. She scared, that's all. She's never been loved. She needs someone to give her a chance ..."

'"Oh, aye," says I. I were beginning to get the idea, you see, Tam, and I weren't sure I liked it.

'Well, we got there. A home for retarded children. It were like a cross between a prison and a hospital and a – a bloody monkey house. Long grey corridors with tiny little windows all closed off wi' bars. All spit and polish and stinking o' pee and disinfectant. And the staff – I'd expected nannies and Sunday school teachers but this lot were prison warders. All rules and orders and everything in its place. But there were no place for love there. No time for it. The kids were wandering up and down the corridors like lost souls crying and wailing and screaming and jabbering to 'emselves. I can't describe it, Tam – it were awful.

'Little girl weren't used to folk, so they'd had to put her away on her own in a single bedroom. That's what they called it, anyhow. Concrete walls. Iron bed. Pot under the bed. You could smell it down the corridor. It were a cell.

'"In there," says Ali.

'There's a peek hole in the door so I peeks in it. A little girl sitting in the corner. No life in her. Dead face, lost eyes, staring at nothing. I made a little noise but she didn't move. I made a louder noise; nothing. She was pretending she weren't there – pretending to me and to everyone else and to herself even. And believing it. She'd never been beaten, she'd never been locked in a cellar, she'd never been bombed and trapped under the rubble for a week all on her own. And at that very second she wasn't sitting there frightened out of her wits in a concrete cell wi' an old farmer spying on her. None of it had happened because she didn't exist. That was the game, you see; that was how she survived.

'Well, we got nurse to open door, and in I goes. Still nothing; she might have been made o' stone. I got closer; nothing. Then I leaned forward sharpish and touched her shoulder – and then I saw her. Her eyes jumped. She couldn't look right at me – she were too scared for that. But her eyes flashed over me shoulder – and then back to the ground for a second. In that second I saw the way she really were. It were all pretence. She knew everything that was going on – everything. And she were terrified.

'I went up to my daughter, Tam, and I said, "I've got a farm to run."

'"She's never had a chance in life, Dad," says Ali. "She needs love and time and she'll come right but in here she's just going to rot. Don't you think she deserves ..."

'"I've got a bloody farm to run," says I. And I turns round and I walks out. Alison follows me for the first hundred yards or so but she soon gives that up. I were furious. I walked to the train station and made me own way back. As if I had time – as if I had the experience – as if I could take the responsibility to care for a child like that! I got back to Thowt It and sent that young man on his way wi' a flea in his ear. And I got on wi' me own life.

'I tried to, anyways. I couldn't get that girl outta my head. I kept thinking – what lay behind the fear? And I kept thinking what a dirty deal she'd had. She'd had a dirty deal being born, a dirty deal brought up locked away, a dirty deal being bombed out and a dirty deal again wi' nowhere but that – that prison cell to go to. And I thought how hard it was that there was no one to give her that one chance to come out right.

'I thought about all that for over a month. Then I went back.

'Nothing had changed. Sitting in same corner, not moving, dead to the world, lost to herself. So I joined her. I went in the cell wi' her. I ate in there. I slept in there. Didn't press her, mind – just got close enough to give her food, or to mop up after her. And all the time I talked to her – told her about the farm and what I did there and how I wanted her to come and live wi' me. I got some books in and read to her; I got some toys in and played with 'em and left 'em lying about, hoping she'd take an interest. But there were nothing. The whole time she never gave the slightest sign she knew I were there. Never so much as glanced at the toys. Just sat there, or lay down. She wouldn't even eat her food if anyone were watching. I had to go out at mealtime. When I came back she'd be sitting in the same position, only her plate would be empty ...

'And I kept looking at her eyes and trying to see something there – something I could relate to. But I never could.

'After a few days my neighbour Tom Capps who was looking after livestock for me began ringing up – "When you coming back, Nutter – I've got me own place to run," he says.

'"Oh, one o' these days, Tom," says I. But I knew I had to go. At the end of a week there were still nothing – not a wink, not a little smile, not a glimmer. And I thought, I've done what I can. Little lass has been given a tiny chance, and she weren't able to take hold of it. Leastways I'd tried.

'In the end I come up close for one last try. This time, there's no flash of the eyes, not even that. And I thinks, here's a change. But what? Is the fear getting further away – or is it her disappearing altogether?

'"Lass," I says, "I've got to go. I can't leave farm any longer. I don't want to leave you here. I want to take care of you. I want to live with you. Will you come? Do you understand me?"'

Mr Nutter shook his head. 'Not a twitch. I'd begun to think she hadn't even heard, let alone understood, and I thought, it's all been wrong, there's nothing there to come out.

'"You have to show me, lass," I said. "You have to show me that there's something there. Will you come?" I said. I held out my hand, like this' – Mr Nutter held his hand out palm uppermost – 'and I waited. One last minute.

'She didn't look up; her eyes stayed the same – lost, empty eyes. In her face nothing. But, Tam ... as I waited her little hand crept up, slow ... slow ... as if it were someone else's ... and she laid her hand in mine.'

Mr Nutter closed his hand.

'And now look at her – it's a miracle!' exclaimed Mrs Pickles fervently.

'Hard work, it were,' said the farmer. 'But slowly – very slowly at first – things began to happen. It were Winnie that began it. Winnie sort of adopted her – she's been more a parent to May than I have. Took to following her around and keeping her out of trouble. May did as she told her. She could take if off a dog, you see, because no dog had ever beaten her like folk had. Winnie taught her everything – where she could go, where she couldn't go. Even showed her where to go t'toilet – by the roadside same as she did.' Mr Nutter chuckled. 'When she took her into kennel at nights, I thought – well, why not? So I built that big de luxe model, and she prefers it to house to this day. Inside reminds her of things, I guess.

'I didn't do owt, just left 'em to it. Spoke kindly to her, gave her food, made sure she knew I loved her and that I'd always be there for her. But I couldn't touch her – still can't. She held my hand in that cell – the bravest thing anybody ever did, that was – but bar that I've not laid a finger on her in four year.

'Next thing was, as she came out of her shell, we found out what was inside. Not a sweet, shy little thing as you might a thought – but a raging tiger!' Mr Nutter laughed. 'Oh, aye – once she found herself, she were furious – smashed up everything she could find! I let her have the run of the place and she made the most of it. Cost me a fortune. I didn't have a dinner plate left by the time she'd done. Oh, she's a fighter all right, is May. But I'd made up my mind I weren't fighting back. I took no notice. I knew it were show, most of it. She could have run away if she'd wanted to, you see, but she never did. She were trying me out. She knew how to love – I'd seen that by that time; but she couldn't trust. Trust has been the hardest thing for her. Other folk didn't see it like that, mind you. I had police up here threatening me if I didn't lock her up. They thought I was off me rocker, letting a maniac like her run wild. Thought she'd kill someone. I remember P.C. Dodd nearly going off his rocker over it. I were standing in the kitchen ankle deep in china and he were spluttering and shouting, eyes popping out of his head. Well, I just picked up teapot – it were about all there were left – and I threw it on floor and I told him – if I decided to smash my place to bits that was my business and if my May wanted to help me, that was hers. He didn't like it but there were nowt he could do about it.

'And then that began to get better too. She began to help me about farm, began to speak, began to play games. Started coming back to what she should be. And in the meantime we've had doctors and nurses and psychiatrists and Health Workers and they've all said the same thing. "She needs professional care," they said. "She needs to go into a home, she's ill, she'll get worse and worse. What's your treatment, what's your theory?" they wanted to know. And I said, "Love." They laughed. But May got better and better, not worse and worse. Then they stopped laughing and then they stopped talking and then they stopped coming altogether and just let us get on wi' it.

'"Congenitally retarded" they said – congenitally unloved, say I. She's as bright as a button! In another few year she'll be as right as rain. Now you see, Tam, why when I saw her holding your hand in the milking shed this morning I could have thrown my hat in the air. She's trusted that dog all this time. Now she trusts you. You're the first person she's let near her since.'

Outside May was playing with a skipping rope. They heard her counting to the rhythm of the rope on the flags.

'My mother likes my made-up mustard,' she chanted. She didn't know the second part and went over and over it. Finally she got fed up with it and began playing tug-of-war with the rope with Winnie. Girl and dog whirled around and around, shrieking and growling.

Inside, Mrs Pickles began to clear up the breakfast things. Tam wanted to go out and play but he felt shy of May now – as if his knowledge of her past made her a different person. But then she caught sight of him and Mr Nutter watching her out of the window. She flung down the rope and came running round. A minute later she stood in the kitchen door with her face all screwed up and glared at Mr Nutter.

'He lives here now,' she stated, nodding at Tam. Having got it out she stopped looking cross and looked worried instead.

Mrs Pickles pursed her lips. 'He'll have a place of his own somewhere,' she insisted.

'God knows where he came from and that's enough for me,' repeated Mr Nutter. May stared from one to the other anxiously.

'Even God doesn't send boys from nowhere,' snapped Mrs Pickles. 'Where's your sense of responsibility, Sam?' she pleaded. 'He'll have parents, relations – people who are worried about him ...'

'I've got no parents,' said Tam quickly. It was true – for the time being.

'He's May's first friend. She needs him and he needs her. Would you prefer him in a home?'

'I wouldn't wish a home on anyone,' said Mrs Pickles quickly.

'Then it's settled. This is your home now, Tam – for as long as you need it.'

'And now you're the luckiest boy in Cawldale,' said Mrs Pickles. And she gave him a shy little smile.

May's face lit up. She skipped quickly across the floor to Mr Nutter, flung her arms around his neck and planted a wet kiss on his cheek. Tam saw Mrs Pickles open-mouthed with astonishment, so surprised she fumbled her pile of dishes and had to snatch to stop them falling.

'I told you,' said May triumphantly to Tam. 'You'll be all right now,' she promised. Then she got suddenly self-aware, darted a nervous glance at Mrs Pickles and shot out again.

Mr Nutter wandered off to his corner under the old clock and blew his nose.

Mr Nutter went out to get on with his work and Mrs Pickles said, 'You're an orphan now, Tam, and you have to work for your keep. You can help with the washing-up for a start.'

While they worked she chatted to him about the farm, about Cawldale, about May – how she weed in the milk churn and Mr Nutter sent the milk to the dairy without knowing, how she got into the hen-house and smashed the eggs and let the hens out and the fox in; how P.C. Dodd came up to check on her and she bit him on the leg. Mrs Pickles seemed to have accepted Tam now and didn't bother him with any more questions about where he came from.

They fell silent as they finished the dishes. Tam glanced out of the window. The sun had gone in and cool, wet air was moving down the valley. He wanted to be outside, helping on the farm, playing with May. He still wanted to get back to his own time, but perhaps not yet. Time and events had made his home distant. Despite the terrors of the day before he was beginning to think of this place as his own. He was needed here.

Even as he thought that he thought of his mother. She needed him too.

Outside the rain began to fall. The odours of the farm rose into the air as the yard got wet – dust, manure, chickens, pigs, hay, straw.

'Just a shower,' remarked Mrs Pickles, glancing out of the window. Already blue sky was coming back further up the valley.

As they began on the pots and pans, darkness fell across the window. Tam looked up – and then glanced anxiously at Mrs Pickles.

It was Rosey.

Tam tried to look as if nothing was happening. He remembered that awful moment in the farmyard when he realised that Mr Nutter could not see her. How real she had been then – and how real she was now, helpless in the rain, letting it fall on her hair and her rags, letting it drip down her face and flow in little dirty streamlets past her mouth and eyes. Her gaze was down to the ground, lost to the world.

'The blue sky is coming back,' said Tam, nodding at the window.

Mrs Pickles looked up from the potato pot. 'Aye,' she said. She looked back down to her work.

Tam tried again. 'Do you get many – many beggars up here?' he asked her, nodding slightly at the window.

Mrs Pickles looked up and frowned slightly. 'Not so many. Why d'you ask?'

'No reason ...' He had seen her eyes; they had passed through the old woman as if she were the wind. Mrs Pickles saw nothing.

What had happened to Rosey? Had she been

bombed or beaten or trapped – what made her so lost? Would she be a mother or grandmother with a job and a car and a nice house and a life and loves of her own if things had been a little different?

The old woman was getting really drenched now. Tam suddenly wanted to go out and take her by the hand, take her into the warm dry kitchen, give her something to eat, shelter her, take care of her. But he didn't move. Mrs Pickles would see. She would see a mad boy take no one by the hand, offer bread to no one, talk to no one, look after no one.

So Rosey stood there, the water flowing freely now over her face, falling in rapid drops from her dangling fingertips and from the ratty ends of her hair – standing there not looking, but to be seen. And Tam stood and stared back from the inside, wiping at a pot with his tea towel, as useless as she was, wanting to help but not daring to admit she was even there.

## Chapter 8

Pigs to feed, chickens to feed, cowshed to muck out, horses to brush down, vegetables to weed ... If Cawldale thought May ran wild they didn't know what work was. For the next couple of days it was one job after another. She showed Tam how to brush the horses and clean their hoofs, how to link up the machinery to the tractor and then hang on the back when Mr Nutter went out to the fields. She showed him how to creep up on rabbits with Winnie as they nibbled at the vegetable patch and to stop her running at them too soon. Even so, she never caught one.

'Too fat,' said May.

Every few hours everything stopped and they all gathered together in the kitchen for something to eat – bread and cheese, or cake, a big bowl of soup or a casserole in the evening that Mrs Pickles cooked. Then it was back to work.

In between jobs there were other things to do. May and Tam rode Spot the pig round the yard a few times while they were waiting for Mr Nutter to make up the swill. Later, she got a ladder to see the white owls in the roof. Tam saw one like a tiny hooded woman staring at him out of the shadows and he felt the air from her wings on his face when she flew off. Two chicks sitting on a beam were just getting their adult feathers and they were half owl, half fluff. They opened their beaks and hissed like cats when they got too close.

May showed him where the geese hatched their eggs in the hedge by the Scots pines behind the orchard. They had to run from the gander. He chased them, hissing like the devil, all the way across the orchard with the goose and her long train of little grey goslings hurrying after.

'Wait till Christmas!' threatened May. She wasn't really frightened and showed Tam how to scare him off by pretending to be a bigger goose with a long neck by stretching out her arm and hissing back. The geese looked at them in fright and they chased them right back across the orchard, laughing at the silly things running as fast their little legs could go, peering backwards over their shoulders and honking indignantly. When Tam told May he'd never eaten a goose she made Mr Nutter promise to kill one for dinner the next day.

'It's the nicest thing to eat there is,' she claimed, slobbering. Tam never thought for a moment about going back home.

Shortly after lunch on that first day, P.C. Dodd paid a call.

They saw him cycling up the drive and ran to hide in the barn. Rosey caught the sense of panic and came after them and all three hid behind the door and listened as he raved at Mr Nutter.

'Two of 'em up here, it's not safe,' he yelled. 'This is a farm, not a nut-house, you need a licence to run a nut-house. Someone'll get hurt, you mark my words. She ought to be locked up, out of harm's way.'

''Appen,' said Mr Nutter calmly.

'Never mind your "'appens",' shouted the policeman. 'What about this ...' He rolled up his shirt sleeve and showed his arm. Even from where he was hiding, Tam could see the black bruise and the little red oval.

'Did you do that?' he asked May.

She smiled. 'I won't do it again,' she promised. 'Policemen taste horrid ...'

'I could catch summat off that. Any other child'd get the seat of their pants beat till dust flew.'

'Our May's a bit different, you understand,' said Mr Nutter.

'Different? A bit different?' yelled P.C. Dodd. 'You can say that again – she's a raving bloody lunatic, that's what she is. She's not safe. And now you've got another one up here – nicking our lad's clothes off line, getting into fights. Supposing she'd come along and bit one of them lads – she could take a finger off!'

'As for Tam,' said Mr Nutter, 'he got lost. He's a sensible lad. You can work out for yersel it weren't him began fighting.'

'Aye, well, I don't like the look of him. There's something not right with that 'un. You've no business bringing outsiders here, not when they're like that. Filling place up wi' lunatics ...'

Mr Nutter went into the house and came out with a paper parcel – the clothes Tam had pinched off the line.

'Them's lad's clothes as went from line and there's ten shilling fer his mum. Tell her it won't happen again.'

'It better not,' threatened the policeman. 'I'll tell

you, Sam Nutter, I've seen enough to get both o' them stuck away where they belong – somewhere you'd never get 'em out, not if you 'ad a division of tanks behind you. Somewhere where they belong. Escaping down town – running wild wi' no control or discipline, doing as they like. You keep 'em under control, that's all. If I find either of 'em down Cawldale once more ...'

He didn't need to go on.

P.C. Dodd took the clothes and handed over another parcel – Tam's own clothes, which he had dropped when he was caught. Then he got on his bike and went back down the hill.

Mr Nutter looked at the barn.

'You heard,' he said. 'He'll have you locked up if he can, May – and you, Tam. Don't let him!' He went off about his business without another word.

'I used to go regular down town,' said May. 'But I won't do it again. Not now.'

Mrs Pickles came back to cook dinner in the evenings and do the laundry. She did Tam's clothes for him, but got into a bit of a mess with his trainers. She came up with a puzzled look on her face.

'I can't get polish to take to these, Tam,' she complained. She'd tried to shine his trainers up with black shoe polish. Tam told her they were plastic, but she didn't seem to understand.

'I'll leave it on overnight, 'appen it'll soak in,' she said.

She made up a bed for Tam in the spare room but nothing would get May to sleep inside.

'Not all night,' she pleaded. In the end she stayed

in the dog kennel but Mrs Pickles wouldn't hear of Tam sleeping there. He had to wait until she had gone and everything was still before he crept downstairs to go out. He was surprised in the hall by Mr Nutter on his way to bed with a candle. The farmer raised his eyebrows, shook his head and carried on his way.

'I saw nowt,' he said.

## Chapter 9

Next day after breakfast while May was off on her own, Mr Nutter asked Tam to feed the pigs. The swill was warmed up on the stove during breakfast, much to Mrs Pickles' disgust.

'A hot breakfast for the pigs,' she scoffed.

'They like it warm, it smells better,' explained Mr Nutter.

'Smells better!' exclaimed Mrs Pickles. 'Not to me it doesn't!'

The aroma of the swill filled the kitchen, milky and wheaty – almost delicious – if it hadn't been pig-swill and hadn't flopped about in the galvanised bucket full of lumps. A full bucket was too much for Tam and he had to take two halves.

As he turned the corner of the farmhouse to the pigsties Winnie ran up to him.

'Where's May gone, girl?' asked Tam. The dog wagged her tail and went round the corner of the house. It was the first time he had seen her and May apart since he arrived. She was bright and keen, as if she was being taken for a walk. Tam guessed what it meant; his heart sank.

Rosey was waiting for him under the chimney with that dull expression on her half-turned face, as if these goings-on were nothing to do with her. The dog sat by her, almost on her feet, and Rosey let her hand down, as if it were falling from her, and laid it on the dog's head. Winnie turned round to lick the filthy grey hand, turned again to look excitedly at Tam. Her head nodded up and down, up and down – yes, yes, yes, yes, yes ...

Tam turned his face away and hurried on to the pigsties. He had the pigs to feed. After that there were the chickens and the ducks, later on there was the evening milking and a ride on Spot. Then there would be the celebration goose and Mrs Pickles' bramble pie, which she had promised if he and May picked the berries.

Behind him Winnie barked. He took no notice.

The pigs got ludicrously excited when feeding time came. Fat old Sarah the sow waddled up to the trough grunting with pleasure and the piglets squealed and writhed after her, crashing against the trough and halfway up the sty in their excitement, a pink porky wave breaking on the sty wall. Then you poured the swill down to the trough all over the pigs and the gobbling started. Sarah plonked herself firmly under the bucket and began scoffing as fast as possible, almost groaning in pleasure as the warm swill splashed over her head. The piglets squealed and snorted and grunted, gobbling at it, diving in it, splashing in it, licking at it as it dripped off Sarah and even biting her ears in their attempts to get more, first, quicker.

Tam watched. He thought of things to come and things gone. He thought of how empty and sad his house was since his father left to live with another family. He thought of his angry, tired mother who tried so hard. He thought of school, where he was always in trouble these days. And he thought of

Cawldale – not the Cawldale he knew but this other Cawldale that lay below the farm like a shadow, full of angry, suspicious people who didn't trust him, didn't like him, people who thought he was all wrong. Then he thought of Thowt It as he had known it before – the broken walls, the grass growing where the floors now were, all traces of home or living gone from the place.

What had happened to it? When?

Tam watched until all the swill was gone and the pigs, unsure of what was going on but certain they hadn't had enough, began looking up at him hopefully.

'One more load to come,' promised Tam. He picked up the bucket and headed back to the house to get the next load.

They were still there, waiting. Winnie had stopped wagging her tail and was watching him closely as he crossed the yard. Tam felt their eyes on him as he walked. He stopped suddenly, full of rage.

'It's your fault,' he shouted at Rosey. 'Why didn't you just leave me alone?' Rosey gave no sign that she had heard him, or even that she knew he was there. She was gazing out across the little valley to the cows scattered on the pasture below the ridge. But then she laid her hand once more on the dog's head and half turned to show Tam one of those shy, sad little smiles.

Tam put down his bucket and took a couple of steps over to pat Winnie's head. 'What do you want with me?' he asked. Winnie wagged her tail and licked his hand. Tam would have loved to turn on his heel and walk away but he knew he couldn't –

couldn't desert his mother for one thing, couldn't trust this new world for another.

'Is it time?' he said. He glanced longingly over his shoulder at the farmhouse. 'My clothes,' he said suddenly. 'I must get my clothes. Wait...' he appealed to Rosey. 'Wait for me,' he begged. Rosey inclined her head – was it a nod? Tam decided that it was. He turned and ran off into the house. He saw Mr Nutter looking surprised in the kitchen, drinking tea, as he dashed past and upstairs to the bedroom. Mrs Pickles was already gone. His clothes, beautifully laundered by Mrs Pickles, lay folded neatly on the chair by his bed and his black trainers, sticky with the polish that Mrs Pickles still hoped would sink in, were on the floor underneath. Tam picked them up. Then he made his way back down, slowly. He paused at the kitchen door. Mr Nutter looked at the clothes under his arm.

'Thank you for – thank you for looking after me,' said Tam.

'Tha's welcome – there's no one I'd rather have.'

Tam couldn't bring himself to say goodbye. He turned abruptly and ran back outside. He had one more thing to do before he left.

He found May where she always was when she wasn't with Winnie – lying in the barn with Spotty pig. The pig lay on her side as if she were feeding piglets and May lay with her head on her enormous tummy, her hands folded behind her head, gazing up at the roof where the rats and mice scurried and crawled across the great crooked beams to their nests in the hayloft.

Tam ran up and put his arms round her. May

stiffened, but then she relaxed and squeezed him back.

'What's the matter?' she whispered anxiously.

Tam said nothing.

'You're my friend,' said May.

Tam left her and ran back out. He could see her sitting up and peering at him over the arc of the pig's belly and for a moment he thought she would follow him. But then she lay back down. Tam walked back to the gable end.

'I'm ready now,' he said.

Winnie stood up to meet him. Tam bent to pat her. The sour, unpleasant smell of the old beggar woman filled his nostrils. He took a couple of steps and was about to walk into the wall, into the future, when there was a noise behind and Mr Nutter appeared.

'I knew you weren't no ordinary child when I saw you walk out of that wall wi' dog three days since, like it were just a thick mist,' he said. 'Goodbye, Tam – don't forget us. And wherever it is you're going to, do what you can for our May, won't you?'

Tam nodded, although he could do nothing.

Mr Nutter smiled. 'And don't keep our Winnie for too long – May relies on her still – all the more since you're to be leaving us.'

'She brought me here,' explained Tam.

'Oh, aye? It doesn't surprise me. She brought our May back to the world, taught her how to trust. Now she's found a friend for her, even though she had to go out of the world to find one. I wonder how far she had to look before she found thee, Tam?'

Tam looked at the dog. Is that what it was, after all? 'I'm just ...' He was about to say that he was nothing special, but then the ground under him seemed to turn to mud.

Cold. Everything moved – the ground under his feet, the wall under his hands, as he fell forward and reached out to stop himself from going down – even the air around him seemed to slur and slip out of his reach. He gasped for air, grasped around him for something to hang on to and then there he was, in the black ashes of the old fires in the ruined fireplace. Behind his head, cold, hard stones. Some sheep were running away out of what had been the kitchen. The wind blew. All around, the long, low remains of the walls like gravestones for the dead house.

Rosey was next to him, crawling slowly on all fours like a big, broken insect. Her face was twisted as if she were in pain, but she made no sound. Behind his head, a bark, muffled and fading. But Winnie was nowhere to be seen. She had taken them back, but she had remained behind with her darling May.

Tam got up. He gave an arm to Rosey and she clawed up him and immediately moved away. Tam took a step after her but then stopped. She turned to watch him, a lingering gaze. But Tam had already forgotten her. At the floor by his feet was his bundle of clothes – his clothes for now.

It was time to go home.

Tam took off the shirt and the overalls, put his own clothes back on. But he tucked the old clothes out of sight, behind some stones loose in a wall. He might need them again. Then he stopped and listened intently for a trace of what had been.

There was nothing left, not even a ghost of a voice.

Grass grew out of the walls. A handful of meadow pipits squeaked and fled over the foundations of what had been the barn. Tam felt disgusted with the emptiness of the place. Only the old woman remained.

Tam began to run up the ridge, panicky for a moment that he might look down to the town and see something else again, but it was all there as it should be – the tarmacked bridge, the greenhouses shining in the allotments, the cricket pavilion, the plastics factory spilling pale smoke over the town.

Tam ran down the hill.

He would have run straight home – he meant to – but there was something going on by the river. A group of people including some policemen were gathered on the bridge watching something going on in the water. Tam had to cross the bridge himself and he paused to have a look, leaning over to look down.

There was a frogman in the water. He was standing among the rushes in the shallows with a tank of air on his back and a mask on his face, and he kept bending over and putting his face in the water. Then he waded out of the reeds to the deeper water and he went under, lying on the water and going down head first. Tam saw his flippers in the air before they slid down after him. In a minute he resurfaced and stood up to his waist in water pulling the mask up his face.

Tam was so engrossed he didn't notice the people on the bridge looking curiously at him. Then the frogman caught sight of him. He pointed and tried to shout but he still had his mouthpiece in and all he could do was give a muffled grunt. He seemed terribly excited. Tam looked around to see what he was pointing at. Then the frogman pulled the mouthpiece away.

'It's the boy, it's the boy,' the frogman was shouting.

## Chapter 10

'Tam – if you're not ready to tell us what happened then I think I can understand that. But you do realise we've all been terribly worried about you, don't you?'

'I know,' said Tam. 'I've been through all this with Mum and Dad, I know, I know,' he repeated.

Mrs Caradine peered into his face as if she could read the secret there. On the sofa his father and mother – he leaning back against the cushions, she perched nervously on the edge of it, both pale and frightened. Tam wanted, wanted, wanted to stop them worrying but he couldn't do it. If he told the truth no one would believe him.

'I was all right,' he repeated for the tenth time. 'I wasn't in any danger. I was looked after ...'

'By whom? Can't you tell us who you were with?' begged his mother.

Tam closed his eyes. If only all this could be over, if only they'd leave him alone.

'You must have done something in three whole days,' snapped his mother, exasperated. 'You had the whole country out looking for you, do you realise that?'

'Did you run away because you didn't want to spend the weekend with me?' his father asked.

'It wasn't that, honest,' said Tam.

'You know I want you to stay with us, but you don't have to, Tam – I wouldn't want you to think you have to,' said his father.

'But it's not that, I told you,' said Tam desperately. They didn't seem to believe anything he said.

'Did someone take you away?' asked his mother. She spoke very gently, as if she didn't want to alarm him.

'No ...'

Tam realised his mother was trying not to cry. He felt like crying himself. He bit his lip.

'I think we've talked enough for now,' said Mrs Caradine kindly. 'Tam's safe home, that's the main thing.' She stood up and picked up her bag. 'It's nice to have you back, Tam,' she said.

'I'm sorry,' said Tam.

'I know you are,' she said, still smiling. It was the too-nice one. 'Well, goodbye, Tam – I'll look by in a few days. If you want to talk to me ...' She opened her bag and gave him a card. 'You can always get me at that number – or at home, if I'm not in the office ...' She scribbled her home number on the back. 'You may find that the time will come when it's best to talk about it, but for the time being we'd all be better just getting back to normal.'

His mother and father exchanged a glance and got up. 'I'll see you out,' said his mother. All three trooped out of the room and onto the road. Tam could see them talking in undertones on the path outside the house, casting furtive little glances at the window. Quietly he slid out and hid behind the door, listening in and peering through the crack. His mother was biting her lip. She had tears in her eyes.

'... he isn't ready to tell us what happened,' Mrs Caradine was saying. 'We have to respect that, I think.'

'Yes, of course – we must be patient,' his father said.

'What do you think happened to him?' pleaded his mother.

'I've no idea – perhaps he just ran off for a few days and found someone prepared to look after him...'

'But his face ...'

Tam glanced in the mirror by the coat stand. His lips were still split and puffy and his eye had gone a glorious purple and yellow and pink and blue. He smiled at himself, a lop-sided, wry grin.

'Maybe he just got into a fight,' said Mrs Caradine doubtfully.

'It must have had something to do with me coming, I'm sure of it,' said his dad.

'Maybe someone took him off, maybe he ran away, we just don't know,' said Mrs Caradine. 'I don't think there's any point in guessing or blaming ourselves. Whatever happened he seems to have survived it remarkably well. All we can do now is make it clear to him how worried we all were, and that he's loved and that we want to help and hope that Tam will tell us in his own time. In the meantime I'll arrange for him to see a therapist – just in case. I hope to get Dr Rose – she's very good. She may be able to help.'

What a mess – what an awful, terrible mess. Suddenly Tam had had enough. He banged the door and walked out.

'I met a dog,' began Tam.

He told them – about the farm, about Mr Nutter, about May, everything. He got up to the bit about May pinching her dinner off the table and Mr Nutter bending down under the table and then he trailed off. They were looking at him as if he were a ghost.

'Well, Tam, thank you for telling us that,' said Mrs Caradine brightly.

'You don't believe me – that's why I didn't tell you,' said Tam bitterly. 'You know I don't make up tales, do I?' he demanded of his father and mother.

His father took a deep breath. 'People don't – they don't do that sort of thing, do they?' he said lamely.

'But what about Mrs Pickles and Mr Nutter and the rest of them?' He appealed to Mrs Caradine. 'You were brought up here, you know. They're all real people, aren't they? Aren't they?' he begged, in a sudden panic that it might be all like they supposed, nothing at all, a story.

'Oh, yes, they're all real,' said Mrs Caradine.

'He talks a lot to Eveline next door about how things used to be,' said his mother quickly.

'You can prove it – it must be real,' insisted Tam.

'Tam, we all have to be patient. Anyone could find out those things – it means nothing. I'm sorry.'

Mrs Caradine smiled crookedly and said goodbye. She got out her keys and opened the car.

Inside she wound down the window. 'Do you know, Tam, that Mrs Pickles is still alive?'

Tam watched her watching him.

'She's a very old lady, now – over ninety. I visit her sometimes. She lives in the old folk's home up on School Lane. You might have seen her yourself – she sits on the lawn on sunny days and feeds the birds.

Tam had seen an old lady like that – sitting on a wicker chair in the sun with a headscarf on throwing crusts to the pigeons and jackdaws. He remembered – she had waved to him once when he walked past. But she didn't look anything like Mrs Pickles.

'She never married Mr Nutter, then?' he asked.

Mrs Caradine gave him a queer look. 'No. The fire put a stop to all that.'

'Fire?' asked Tam.

'Didn't you know? Ah, there, you don't know everything about Thowt It, then,' she laughed. 'That's how the farm got destroyed. It was a terrible fire by all accounts. Mr Nutter died in it.'

Tam got a lump in his throat. 'And May?'

'I don't know about her. It was all before my time, really. Ask Mrs Pickles, she'll know. She won't mind. She likes a bit of company.' Mrs Caradine smiled her toothy, professional smile, wound up the window and drove off.

Back in the house Tam's mother went to cook dinner and he and his father sat watching TV. But his mother came in suddenly and knelt by his side, holding his hand, looking up at him.

'I know you don't want to talk about it, Tam – but I thought you were dead. I want you to promise that you'll do everything you can not to let it happen again.'

But the fire. The broken walls of the farm. He had been thinking – he could go back and warn them. He could save their lives.

His mother bit her lip and waited. Tam said nothing.

It was hard. His mother was polite and tender to him as if he might disappear if she got cross. His father stayed another couple of days and didn't dare take Tam away even though he begged him to – not that he wanted to go, but just to prove that he wouldn't run off. His father came to stay at weekends instead. They had what should have been a great time – fishing, seeing films, doing things. But it wasn't the same. Sometimes Tam would forget why all this was going on but then he would catch his father giving him an odd, curious, half-afraid look, and Tam would remember. He was a problem child.

At school he caught the teachers looking at him the same way, as if he was ill. Once a week there was the therapist, Dr Rose. She was nice enough, but Tam couldn't see the point. They just sat and talked for an hour about all sorts of things, except what the problem was. She asked him once at the beginning to tell her the story he had told his parents and Mrs Caradine, which he did. She never mentioned it again. Sometimes she gave him tests but she never told him how he did.

His friends didn't seem to mind so much but the news filtered through to them, too. One or two at school called him Loony Tam. His good friends didn't do that but even they were different with him – as if they didn't really know him, as if he lived in another world. That was truer than they would ever know, but he never told them that he had travelled back in time.

He saw nothing of Rosey. After he left her up at the ruins of Thowt It she didn't show up in the town.

No doubt she had gone back. Tam envied her, because he missed them all – Mr Nutter, May, those days working and playing – like a golden dream lost forever. He had a life to live here in the present, but Rosey had no life anywhere.

Up there on the hills were the broken walls, the rotting charred beams. Once, Tam dug down beneath the turf and found, under a few centimetres of soil, black ashes. Those ashes were the kitchen table, the clock on the wall, the rugs on the floor, the floor itself, the whole life at Thowt It Farm. Mr Nutter had died in that fire. His ashes were here too. When did that fire burn? There was so much he wanted to know. What of Winnie? And what of Rosey – was she part of that wet black under the grass where she had walked? Most of all, what had happened to May? Maybe all that was left of May lay here too, between the walls where the sheep now grazed. Mrs Caradine hadn't known if May escaped or not. But she had told Tam where to find out.

Mrs Cranshaw at the Beckside Home for the Aged did not like boys coming to visit her old ladies and gentlemen. She said it disturbed the old folk but the truth was, it disturbed Mrs Cranshaw. Mrs Cranshaw had a routine and Tam wasn't in it. He wasn't a relative and Mrs Cranshaw knew for a fact that people in general and boys in particular, never, ever visited old people they weren't related to.

'What have you got to do with Mrs Pickles?' she demanded.

'I think I met her once,' said Tam.

'Nonsense,' declared Mrs Cranshaw firmly. 'Mrs

Pickles has been in this home for nearly twenty years. You've never been in here and she never goes out. You're up to something. Go on – clear off!' She shooed him towards the door.

'I want to visit her,' insisted Tam. 'Mrs Caradine said she'd like to see me.'

'Mrs Caradine!' That explained it. A nosy social worker tiring out her ladies with their good turns again. It made the social workers feel good but it didn't do anything for anyone else – especially Mrs Cranshaw. She told Tam to wait and banged the door loudly as she went off to have a word with Mrs Pickles.

'You can go through – it's the red door on the left,' she said gruffly when she came back. Tam trotted off down the corridor. 'Don't be long and don't tire her out and no tricks!' shouted Mrs Cranshaw after him. A couple of old gentlemen trying to watch telly in the lounge shushed crossly at her. Mrs Cranshaw blushed and went to hide in her office. She knew she shouldn't have let that boy in, he was causing trouble already.

Mrs Pickles was old, older than anyone Tam had ever seen. She sat in a tall chair with a blanket over her straight bony legs. She was very frail and pale and very thin, and she trembled slightly as she sat there, like a leaf in a slight breeze. She spoke in a twittering little voice quite unlike the cross tones that Tam remembered. Indeed, she looked so different that Tam doubted that she was the right one. She asked him politely to sit down opposite her and she began to talk – what a pleasant surprise it was to be visited by a young person, how kind it was of Mrs Caradine to get Tam to come and call, how she hoped he wouldn't be bored, how one of the nurses would bring them a cup of tea and a slice of cake in a minute – and all the time her eyes flickered to and fro – at his shoes, out of the window, across at the wall. Anywhere but at his face.

'Mrs Caradine said you used to work up at Thowt It Farm during the war,' said Tam at last.

'Yes, yes, that was a long time ago,' said Mrs Pickles nervously. She glanced away and picked at the beads around her neck. 'I'm beginning to feel tired already, dear – I get so terribly tired these days. I'm over ninety years old, did you know? I think you might have to go now ...' She glanced at her watch and then Tam was certain it was Mrs Pickles, his Mrs Pickles because she suddenly began tutting and clicking her tongue, a rapid little burst of disapproval, just as she used to do.

Tam glanced up at the clock that she had hanging on her wall. It was a battery one with no tick at all, but it would do. He nodded at it. 'That old clock's gone off its head again,' he said, in a broad accent.

She stared at him. Her mouth worked, her hand hovered trembling at her throat. Tam thought she was going to deny it. He opened his carrier bag and took out his black trainers.

'That polish still hasn't sunk in yet,' he said.

Mrs Pickles stiffened and stared at the shoes, her eyes round with fright. Then she closed her eyes and sighed. When she opened them she looked at him closely for the first time.

'I knew it was you, Tam,' she said shakily. 'I knew it was you weeks ago when I saw you walking past the lawn and I waved at you.'

'I didn't know you, then,' replied Tam. 'It was before.'

'I wondered if you'd come. I thought of you a lot over the years – and Thowt It Farm and dear old Sam Nutter. Wasn't he the nicest man you ever met, Tam?' She peered at him, a trembling smile on her face.

Tam smiled back and nodded. Yes, Mr Nutter was the nicest man.

'The best man who ever lived,' said Mrs Pickles fervently. 'They all thought he was crazy. Well, it's all gone now, hasn't it – Sam and his Alison. She died in the war – bombed, they said. And poor May. She was heartbroken when you went, Tam. Poor child. She was good to Sam those last months, though – sat on his lap, cuddled him, made a fuss of him – just like any other little girl. Now only I'm left ...' Her eyes had gone red and she dabbed at them with a lacy little hanky she pulled from out of her sleeve. 'We were gong to be married, did you know?' Tam nodded. He felt the sadness of it – her sorrow at losing her Sam still fresh in her after half a century.

'People said I wanted him for the farm, but that wasn't it at all,' she went on, suddenly sounding cross again and quite like her old self. She began to go on about how folk gossiped, but then stopped suddenly and started, full of fright again.

'It gives me the colly-wobbles looking at you, Tam,' she said. 'You haven't changed – not a hair different and fifty years gone by. Give me your hand…' Tam gave her his hand and she gave it a cool, shaky squeeze. 'Flesh and blood, just as before,' she muttered. 'Sam knew you were something different – not an ordinary boy. Even I thought he was crazy, then, but he was right about that like he was right about all the other things …'

'But I am ordinary,' said Tam. 'I live here.' Then he told her about moving here from London, about how Winnie came and fetched him and about Rosey, about getting stuck and how he got back.

'I told them, but they think I'm mad,' said Tam. 'I have to go and see a therapist and everything.'

Mrs Pickles laughed. 'You can't blame them,' she pointed out.

'But now I have you – you'll help me tell them, won't you?'

Mrs Pickles pursed her lips. 'I'm sorry, Tam. They wouldn't believe me, either. Old folk and young folk – the ones in the middle never believe them. It just won't work. Take my advice. Make up a story – tell them you got lost, or someone kidnapped you or anything but the truth. Make them happy. They'll never believe the truth. They never believe anything unless you wave it under their noses. I know; I was the same. All these years I thought you were just a boy on the run in the war. But here you are …' she nodded and sighed tiredly.

Tam asked the question that he was dreading. 'What happened to them – Mr Nutter and May?' he begged. 'Mrs Caradine said there was a fire …'

'You don't know?' she said. 'Yes, it was the fire that finished it. No one ever found out how it started – no one even knew it was happening until the whole place was alight. Tucked away up there in that little valley...

'I saw it myself, late at night. I heard the fire engines and I looked out of the window – my little terrace had a view up that hill and you could see it by then – when it was too late. Sparks going up, clouds of sparks in the dark. The tips of the flames leaping right up above the ridge, as if the hill was on fire. And a dirty orange stain on the sky from the fire and smoke. I went running up there, of course, and so did a lot of other people, but it was too late, too late. Mr Nutter died in his bed. He never felt anything by all accounts – choked on the fumes as he slept.

'As for May, well, she was in the kennel, as usual, It was a few months after you left. She was heartbroken, you know, but Mr Nutter kept promising her you'd come back if you could. She was badly burned when we got there and in the most terrible state – raving, screaming, hysterical. There were sparks everywhere and the heat was tremendous – the whole place was burned to the ground and all the outhouses went up. She may have got caught by some falling timber – that's what people said, but I think she went in to try and get him out. Poor thing, she didn't stand a chance. Even the firemen couldn't do a thing – just stood there waiting for it to finish while everything went up in flames. Poor May, she was getting on so well, but that fire finished it all off for her. They'd had to lock her in a van to stop her running into the flames. All that hard work, all that loving, all gone down the drain. Poor Sam. Of course they all laughed at me when I said she'd tried to save him – she was just a lunatic to them. The policeman was there – Doddy. He was convinced she'd started it, kept going on that she should have been locked up years ago. He put all that in his report, I expect. She knew it was all over with her, with Sam dead. Screaming and shouting in that van, with the flames roaring everywhere – "Let me out, let me out ..." No one could do owt with her. So she went to the home after all. It would have broken Sam's heart if he'd have known. Poor lamb, she knew what was coming. She'd heard him talking about it often enough. She was so well, wasn't she, Tam? – bright as a button. All gone.

'I went to see her a few times, but she was nothing to what she had been. Full of drugs, couldn't barely stand up. Begged me to take her home, but I couldn't do it. She was getting violent. It was a terrible place, just like Sam said – nasty bare rooms, locked doors, terrible food – but there was nothing else for her. I often wonder how she turned out. Still locked up in some home I suppose. I should have gone to see her more often, but I couldn't bear it. She was getting worse and worse every time and there was nothing I could do ...'

# Chapter 11

Tam, too, could look from his bedroom window up the hill to where Thowt It lay hidden in its secret valley. He spent a lot of time gazing out of his window and imagining what it must have been like on that cold night long ago – imagining the flames that must have appeared to spring out of the hillside, the sparks rising slowly up and then drifting away in the wind, the orange glow of destruction cast up on the clouds.

It was all in the past, all happened and gone. Or was it? Tam wasn't sure, but if he could get back, it might be possible to warn them.

He had it all worked out. He had been missing from home for three days, and he had spent exactly the same time in the past. A day for a day. His father had come to pick him up on Friday; when he arrived, Tam was already back in time at Thowt It Farm. May has rescued him from P.C. Dodd the first night. The next day he had worked on the farm and P.C. Dodd came up to complain. The day after he had spent on the farm, working. The next day he had come back, and it had been Monday morning here, in his own world. A day for a day. If he could find out how long it had been between his leaving Thowt It and the fire, he would know how long he had to get back. If he could get back he could say, on such and such a day there will be a fire, you must not be here …

He asked Mrs Pickles. She could not remember exactly how long had passed after Tam's visit before the fire, but she thought it was something like five or six months. 'It was springtime,' she recalled. She did not think that Tam's plan was possible. In fact, she did not even approve.

'What's done is done,' she said in her shaky voice. But that wasn't true. A boy's suit had disappeared off a washing line ... May had come into the house to her food. P.C. Dodd had been bitten on the arm. None of those things would have happened if he hadn't slipped through that gap in the fireplace.

He had five months – five months to get back and save May, Mr Nutter, the farm. Every day Tam ran up to the ruins, looking for Rosey and for Winnie, but the old beggar woman and her dog did not reappear.

Sometimes when he was sure no one was near he shouted their names, or to Mr Nutter, warning him about the fire, hoping his voice might somehow pass across the divide. And if they did hear, what would change? Would the farm suddenly spring up around him? Would Mrs Pickles suddenly turn into Mrs Nutter and still live here with children who had not been alive a few seconds ago? After he had shouted, Tam dug in the earth; but after a few centimetres, he came across that layer of dark, sad ash.

Once he crept into the fireplace and pressed himself against the stone in the hope that he might suddenly feel that cold sensation and find himself on his backside with the hens squawking and running away from him. But it remained cold and hard, unliving stone with no secrets to tell. After a few weeks Tam began to go less often. The story was too sad for him to want to linger.

Weeks passed; months passed. The summer came and blossomed and died. Tam saw nothing of Rosey or the dog. At home things got better. He didn't take Mrs Pickles' advice and make up a story; he was sure he couldn't keep that up for any length of time, let alone forever. Instead, he pretended to forget. He didn't answer when anyone spoke about it and gradually they stopped asking. They hadn't forgotten. His parents, his teachers, Mrs Caradine, all gazed at him strangely every now and then. But it happened less often. Finally the therapist decided there was nothing wrong with him.

'If he doesn't want to talk about it, we'll just have to put up with it,' she told Tam's mother when she protested. 'There's nothing wrong with him that I can make out – a perfectly healthy young man, mentally and physically.'

'But something must have happened,' insisted his mother.

'To tell you the truth, Mrs Sams, I'm not at all sure that Tam knows himself,' said Dr Rose. 'He may have forgotten. One day it may resurface – but in the meantime, I think it would be wise not to press him about it.'

In this way it became as if nothing had happened. His mother and father never mentioned the missing days. Mrs Caradine never mentioned it. His teachers at school had never spoken about it in the first place. All there was to show him his memory was real were his visits to Mrs Pickles and the shirt and overalls hidden in his room. He soon began to realise that the old lady didn't like to talk about those days with him. He made her feel uncomfortable; he was a ghost. Tam began to feel as Dr Rose had said – as if something completely different had happened, and his imagination had made up the whole thing just to cover up ...

Every Friday Tam and his mother went to the supermarket to do a big shop. It drove him mad – he hated hanging around while she spent ages dawdling over the frozen peas and pickles and the rest of it. His job was to load the stuff into the car and then out to the kitchen back at home

It was a Friday in early winter. The wet brown leaves on the ground had been just a little frosty when they set off, but it was all damp and misty by the time they came back. Mrs Sams pulled up in front of the house and got out to open the boot. Tam came round to join her, but when she stood aside to let him get at the boxes he didn't move. He was staring up the street.

'Tam?' she said.

'Just a minute,' said Tam.

They'd come back. Rosey and the dog. He left the car and walked across the road towards them.

She was the same, she was always the same – her felted hunks of ugly hair hanging over her collar, her hands limp at her sides, her head on its crooked neck tipped towards the ground as if it were too heavy for her, her eyes staring at the ground and moving up and away down the road as he came closer. But Winnie had changed. She crouched down by the old woman's side, all the bright energy drained away from her. When Tam walked up she thumped her tail and licked her lips, but she didn't get up.

Tam bent down to stroke her head. 'Hello, Rosey,' he said brightly.

Rosey looked away as if she hadn't heard. He saw her eyes creep sideways to glance at him and then they slithered away back to the ground. Her head drooped further down; her lips moved, but she made no noise.

Tam glanced over his shoulder. His mother was coming up behind him. He got up and moved to Rosey's side.

'How are they, Rosey?' he begged her. 'Mr Nutter and May – how are they? Please, Rosey ...' But she didn't, wouldn't, couldn't respond. Her eyes drifted sideways to take a glance at Tam's mother who came up now, loud with false friendliness. 'Hello, Rosey, we haven't seen you for a long time,' she shouted, bending close to the old woman's ear.

'She's not deaf,' protested Tam.

'Are you sure?' asked his mother with a half smile. But she was anxious. Tam realised it had been a mistake telling her about Rosey's part in his adventure. Maybe she thought the poor old thing had something to do with his disappearing.

'Are you all right, dear?' his mother was demanding. She took out her purse and fumbled in it. 'We have to go now, Rosey, got to get she shopping in. Here ...' She slid a pound coin between her finger and thumb and held it out. Rosey's hand came floating up to the money. Slowly her fingers closed over the coin and dropped it in a pocket.

'Come on, Tam, let's get it done, you can chat to her some other time ...'

Tam lingered. His mother frowned. 'I see you've got a dog, Rosey,' she said. She bent down to pat Winnie. Tam watched as the animal rolled over and thumped her tail, looked up gratefully for the attention.

'She doesn't seem well, does she?' muttered his mother. 'None too well fed, I expect. Hello,' she said suddenly. 'Look here, Tam – her fur's all singed. Look, my God, she's got half the skin off her side. This dog's been burned ...'

It was too late.

'Look – oh, you poor thing, she must be in agony...'

'Rosey,' said Tam.

'She's covered in blisters. Good girl, good girl, stay still, I won't hurt you ...'

It was too late. It was all lost. Rosey's face was a blank, impossible to read. What had happened? But he saw her eyes steal round to take a sideways glance at him as if she didn't believe he was there, as if he would disappear like everything else she had known in the whole terrible world at the next gust of wind.

'Can't you tell me?' whispered Tam. He wanted so much to know what had happened. He had wanted so much to help and he had done nothing.

'Are you all right, Rosey?' he asked her. He reached out to take her hand to see if she had been caught in the fire too, but Rosey snatched it away and cast one quick, clear, hard look directly at him, that said as clearly as if she had used words: 'Don't touch.' Tam dropped his arm. Rosey's eyes died and drifted down.

'This dog needs to see a vet,' said his mother suddenly. She tried to scoop Winnie up in her arms, but the dog twisted free. 'Come on, come on, girl,' she called. Winnie backed off.

'She has to go to a vet. She's been badly burned – do you understand? She needs treatment,' bellowed his mother at Rosey. Rosey didn't appear to hear. But between her lips she made an odd, clucking noise. And then the dog was off like the wind, straight along the road without a backward glance, away from the three people standing watching her – away from all help up the hill.

'Hey!' Mrs Sams glared at the old woman. 'Well, there's more going on in there than you make out, isn't there, deary? It won't be my fault if the dog dies – I've done what I can. Come on, Tam – shopping. Now!' she added dangerously as she turned to march off back to the car, '... shouldn't be allowed to have dogs ...' Tam heard her muttering to herself.

'Goodbye, Rosey,' he said out loud, and then whispered, 'I'll see you – up at Thowt It.'

He followed his mother to the car and turned to watch the old woman halfway across the road. She was looking straight at him, with the faint, pale ghost, or maybe the very beginnings of a little smile on her tired, dirty face. It faded like a sliver of dirty ice as soon as she saw him looking and she began to drift up the road, after the dog, up to the hill behind the town.

# Chapter 12

Tam went up to the ruined farm later. They weren't there but he knew they were coming. He awoke that night without surprise. A shadow of pale moonlight lay across his bed. He glanced at the clock: 2 o'clock. Outside was silence, but Tam knew that the night was not empty.

They were waiting for him on the pavement opposite. She stood as always, quietly, in the shadows, as if she was there by chance and nothing to do with him. But when he looked out of the window he saw her head move slightly and he knew she was watching him, sneaking one of her shy, secret little glances. She was waiting for him all right. He couldn't see Winnie at first, but in a moment she came out of the shadows by the entrance to the cricket club. She sat on Rosey's feet, leaning sideways against her legs and looked up, wagging her tail slowly at Tam's pale face in the window.

Tam dressed quickly. It was cold out; he put on thick trousers, a pullover. He took out from the cupboard a bag of old clothes – the set of overalls and shirt May had given him. He had taken them down from Thowt It when the weather got bad. His heart was thumping, almost in panic. This was an adventure out of this world. He thought of taking a flask and sandwiches but there was no time – he couldn't keep them waiting out there on the street for him.

All the time Tam was getting ready he was

thinking, 'But I shouldn't, I shouldn't ...' It was dangerous. He might get stuck, he might find himself in the middle of the fire – anything could happen. But he had made a promise to Mr Nutter. There remained the chance, the slender chance despite the dog's burnt fur, despite the ash under the ground, that he could find a way to save Mr Nutter and May, the one from the fire, the other from the home.

He put on his coat, rubber boots and a woolly hat. Before he left, remembering his last stumbling climb up the hill to Thowt It with May, Tam picked up the long rubber torch his mother kept under the sink. He popped it into his bag and then slipped out, closing the latch softly behind him.

Winnie licked his hand; Rosey shuffled away from him as he came close and moved along the path towards the hill. There was no word between them as they made their way past the neat little yards, past the tiny rectangles of earth with their roses and rockeries. Once Tam stopped to pat Winnie's side, she yelped and snapped at the air in front of his fingers. Then he was more careful. There was a raw patch as big as his palm on one side, surrounded by fiery skin and singed fur. As they turned off the road and up the footpath on the hill, the old woman began to pant, her breath harsh with the effort of the climb. The moon was a hard, bright wedge in the sky that lit up the grass and the folds of the hills. Tam had no need of his torch but he was glad he had brought it along. Who knew what sort of night it was to be fifty years past?

The town fell behind them. The wind was on their

backs and Tam could smell the plastics factory, still churning out its pale stink unseen into the night air. Gradually the town became a small pattern of lights in the dark valley below them. The ridge was suddenly there. Tam looked down. The long, low walls of Thowt It Farm lay below like a graveyard in the moonlit pasture.

As they reached the edge of the old farm buildings Tam turned on his torch and explored the walls, with the grass growing out of them, with their crumbling mortar and broken stones. A dozen or more sheep suddenly jumped up and ran away like a rush of wind. They gathered together to sleep in the shelter of the walls. The place looked worse in the torchlight, somehow. Tam was scared.

'Did you see the fire?' he asked Rosey. At the word 'fire' the old woman winced. Tam licked his lips. 'It's no use going back,' he said. 'It's all over.'

Rosey began to move into the fireplace. 'Mr Nutter's dead,' said Tam. 'I can't help.'

The dog limped behind Rosey. Tam followed them.

He'd done it often enough by now to be getting nervous about that giddy, slipping past of time. His stomach lurched, he staggered, but he managed not to fall down. But he and the old woman and the dog were standing together in the same position, in the same darkness, the light of his torch lit up the same patch of wall. It hadn't worked. Then Tam leaned back, the stone behind him was warm. He moved his light and saw the ashes.

Black, everywhere black. The heat from the

stones and the baked earth made the still night warm. The walls were still tall, the windows stared across the valley like blinded eyes. Black scorch marks flared above them and round them and the doors where the blaze had licked. Inside the house, a desert of strewn charred wood and soot. There were ashes, ashes in heaps spilling out of the door, ashes inside, centimetres deep, ashes in drifts against the walls, ashes rising like dust whenever he moved his foot. The heat had cracked the plaster from the walls and one wall had fallen in. Then Tam looked up and saw the stars; the roof had disappeared.

Around were the shells of the outbuildings – the great barn, its walls still rising above the house, a rubble of fallen stone slates inside throwing heat up to the stars – the chicken shed with the charred remains of the birds who had been trapped inside. Ashes and blackness everywhere, and everywhere, silence. When the farm had been alive there had always been some noise, even in the dead of night – cows chewing the cud, sheep or chickens or mice or pigs or ducks or people – always something alive and kicking or calling or eating or just turning over in its sleep. All gone. The only noise was the little wind that passed over the warm stones, stirring the ashes. In this one burning, so many deaths.

Tam moved up to the house and shone his torch through it. There was precious little to recognise. The iron stove that Mr Nutter used to kick still poked through above the mess. He could see a couple of pots and pans still on it and there, on its nail in the wall, Mr Nutter's frying pan with which he had cooked Tam that wonderful bacon and eggs.

Tam felt sick. 'Why did you bring me back here?' he suddenly demanded, rounding on Rosey as if it were all her fault, the deaths, the ashes. Rosey said nothing.

'It's stupid, being here,' cried Tam. His voice rang on the stones of the dead farm. Winnie whined, lay down and rested her head on her paws. Rosey stepped back, her hand on her mouth as if he had done something disgraceful. Tam felt sorry that he had alarmed her. He felt close to the mad old woman – although she said nothing, although she showed no sign of understanding or feeling, she had shared this strange, unaccountable adventure with him.

'I'm sorry, Rosey. Let's go back,' said Tam. 'There's nothing here – let's go back.'

He stepped back towards the fireplace. Winnie followed him, tail low. But the old woman held back.

'Come on,' urged Tam. 'They've gone – there's nothing to do here. We're too late. You came back too late,' he added bitterly.

Rosey lifted her arm and pointed at the farm. Her lips moved, she strained, but no sound came out. Tam watched her excitedly. But although she struggled she couldn't make a sound.

'They're dead,' insisted Tam. 'Mr Nutter. And May might as well be. Don't you understand?'

Rosey's head went down. Her eyes, which had been almost looking at him, sank away. Her lips moved weakly; she seemed to fade. There was nothing to tell after all.

She took a couple of steps away and leaned against a wall, looking down. She looked desperately miserable. Tam felt so helpless.

'I'm sorry, Rosey, there's nothing there any more.' Rosey made no response. Winnie began to whine and began pushing her nose into the old woman's leg as if urging her to get going, but she just leaned there, saying nothing, doing nothing. The dog was persistent. She pushed and pushed and barked, and gradually, Rosey came back to life. She started to amble away but in the wrong direction – away from the fireplace, away from the present, as if she meant to stay here in the past forever. Winnie stood watching Tam, her tail wagging slowly.

'No ...' Tam tried to get in front of the old woman. He was about to say there was nothing for her here, but he realised that there was nothing for her in her own time either. What difference did it make? But for some reason he was reluctant to let her go. She avoided his eye but tried to go round him. Tam grabbed her by the arm. Through her rags he could feel a ridge of bone where her arm had been broken and badly set, long ago.

There was a ridge of bone. Tam felt a violent shock go through him.

Rosey snatched away her arm. Tam grabbed back at her and for a second the two scuffled before she gave up the unequal fight. Tam tore up her sleeve.

Her arm turned inwards, like a crab's.

For a second a blazing hot look was exchanged between the boy and the old woman. Tam saw her eyes full of life on him. He saw the scarred skin on her face, the scars of her terrible effort to save Mr Nutter fifty years ago. Then Tam dropped her arm and backed away.

'It's too late,' he jabbered. 'It's too late ...' And now she knew he knew. The old woman stretched out her hands to him, tipped her head to one side and broke into a pleading, toothless smile, full of hope.

Tam backed away. He was full of anger. 'May's dead!' he screamed, his voice jarring the night. 'She's dead – don't you understand – she died in the fire and now there's nothing left of her – just ashes – just ashes!'

The old woman's hands came up to her mouth and she stared at him in horror. Tam stared back, choking on tears, on fear, on shame. He could not, would not accept what had happened to his friend in the years in between. He could not accept that he owed this old woman anything.

Suddenly her lips opened and she screamed. She screamed silently. Then she turned and staggered past him away – back to everything she had lost, away from the world, away from herself – back to the ashes of her past.

Winnie was on her heels but Tam seized her collar. 'You have to take me back,' he pleaded. The dog stood firm watching the old woman, but she let Tam drag her as far as the portal. She paused at the edge and barked, looking at him, moving her tail.

'I can't stay,' he cried. 'What if I got stuck? What good would it do?' Winnie gave him a long, scornful look. He saw her run off on the heels of the friend to whom she had been so faithful for so long, before his vision blurred and he felt the sliding passage of time around him.

Tam turned from the ruins and walked back down

home. His face was still but inwardly he raged. He felt that he had turned to stone.

'I don't dare go,' he muttered. But he did not believe it.

He was halfway down the first field when he heard a bark behind him; just one. He turned and shone the torch up the hill. He searched for a second before he caught the figure of Winnie standing on top of the wall. When he saw her, she sat down and watched him.

She was waiting. He had one last chance.

Tam began to cry. He cried for himself, for May who was gone forever and at last for poor Rosey too who had lost so much in that fire long ago. In his distress he dropped the torch and as he scanned the skyline to catch sight of the dog he saw how it was all the same. This dark night could be another dark night fifty years ago – the same sky, the same fields and stones, the same dog, the same boy; and of course, the same girl.

He snatched his torch up; the beam shot into the darkness like a searchlight.

'I'm coming,' Tam shouted. 'I'm coming!'

He ran back up the hill.

The charred walls of the farmhouse reared suddenly up. Tam flashed the beam across them, the gaping windows, the blind doors, Rosey – May – was already gone. Winnie was snuffling around, tail high over her back trying to get the scent.

'Where is she, girl? Where's May!' encouraged Tam. The dog looked up and barked, and tried again. Tam remembered how bad she had been chasing rabbits. Winnie was no tracker. She was just looping round and round and finding nothing.

'May! May!' shouted Tam. But there was no reply. His voice died among the broken walls. Tam ran to search in the house. He paused at the doorway and his beam probed into the charred shell.

The torch picked out details of the destruction of the little world up there on the hill. Odd survivors – the charred seat of the big wooden chair Mr Nutter sat in at table jutted out through the remains of the upstairs floor. A couple of spokes from the back survived, sticking up like ribs. A blackened chain hung on a nail on the wall – all that remained of the old clock. Tam held his breath, afraid of disturbing memories or ghosts. He crept into the wreckage. Here was the leg of a table, here a metal box, a door handle, cutlery, an exploded tin can. And there to one side of where the sideboard had once stood was the metal skeleton of an old mattress, burned through to the springs. It had fallen down on the blazing bedroom floor. Was that where Mr Nutter had died?

As he thought of this, Tam was aware of a creak above him and he shone the beam up to heaven. He imagined for a moment that May was up there, hiding in the dark air itself. But then he saw that in one section of the dark sky, the stars were missing. A few beams were still precariously in place, holding up a section of roof. He heard it again – a slow, hard creak. It could come down any minute.

Tam flicked his torch over the wreckage once more, poked in the corners.

'Rosey!' But she wasn't in there. Tam turned and picked his way rapidly back to the door.

Winnie was still running in loops. 'Where is she, girl? Track, track!' said Tam. He glanced longingly at the chimney breast. He would have loved to leave this place where he had no friends, where he was alone and lost. He couldn't; he wouldn't go back alone.

Then Winnie got the scent at last. She barked and headed off into the darkness, up the slope away from the farm to the ridge. She'd gone to town. He'd lost minutes already. Tam despaired. Anything would be better than getting stuck down there again. He just hoped he could catch up. Already the dog was out of sight.

'Winnie!' he shouted. He ran up after her but at that moment he heard feet behind him. He turned, thinking it must be May. A powerful hand grabbed his collar. Tam received a blow on his ear that sent him flat to the ground.

'Looting, are you, you little bastard?' Tam found himself dragged violently to his feet. He just stood there swaying with shock and surprise.

'After old Nutter's money, are you, you thieving little git?' demanded the man.

Tam cringed back and scraped at the ground to retrieve his torch. He couldn't see the man but the man could see him and dealt him another tremendous blow to the head that sent him spinning.

'I was looking for someone,' cried Tam.

The man seized him and pulled him closer by the shirt. 'Souvenirs, bones? Looking for a few bits to keep in a tin box, is that it?'

Tam crouched, ready to take another of those hard blows. The blow never came. There was a guttural, strangled snarl, fast feet on the ashes that suddenly left the ground. Tam caught a glimpse of something dark fighting in the air, something biting and clawing at the man's head, making that frightful savage noise. The man screamed and clawed at it. Tam fled. Behind him the noises stopped; there was no chase. As he came up to the top of the ridge a dark shadow raced up to him. Winnie paused to make sure he was all right.

'Go on, Winnie, good girl,' he gasped. The dark shadow disappeared. Behind them, on the ridge, Tam heard the man give one bellow after them – a shout of pure rage.

Tam didn't stop until he was exhausted. He crouched down behind a stone wall to get back his breath. The man didn't follow, but the dog had disappeared again. Tam was alone. He could not get back. He had to find them – for his sake as well as hers.

As he crouched down out of sight, a pulsing wail filled the night air. Air raid, thought Tam. This was his chance; the streets would be empty. One piece of good luck, he thought. But he was wrong. For a few minutes after the siren the streets would be full of people going to the shelters. It would take ten minutes or more before everything was quiet. He waited only a few seconds before he slipped out from behind the wall and ran down towards the town.

He came out behind the dry stone wall, still there in his own day, that separated the fields from the footpath at the edge of town. Tam checked that all was clear, jumped over and ran up towards the allotments. There, a hundred metres from where the houses began, Winnie rejoined him. He saw her struggling out over the thin wire around the allotments. She whimpered as she caught her wound on the wire and then barked for him. Tam tried to hush her, but she didn't seem to understand the need to be quiet. She ran between him and the gap in the fence two or three times, barking and wagging her tail. May was in the allotments.

'Please, I'm coming,' begged Tam. As fast as he could, to stop the dog barking again, he slithered on his belly under the wire and through the long grass, wet with dew, onto one of the grass paths around the plots. Winnie was standing in front of him. As soon as he was on his feet she ran on.

They ran past two or three plots and then Winnie stopped and began sniffing around in the grass. Tam waited, his heart in a clamour. She snuffled up and down, and then glanced anxiously at Tam.

'Go on, Winnie, find her,' urged Tam. She wagged her tail, but to his dismay she began circling, circling.

She's lost the scent, he thought. The dog ran up to him and then away, uncertainly nosing the grass. Then she began to go back the way they had come. Tam followed closely. In this light, she was out of sight three metres away.

The wailing of the siren had died away. Tam was too far off to hear the people on the streets, chatting as they made their way to shelter. Thinking everyone inside, Tam decided to take a risk. He turned on the torch and flashed it quickly up and down the gardens.

The effect was instantaneous.

He was not alone. 'Hey, you, what d'you think you're doing? Put that light out!' Someone came running down the path towards him. At the same time, Tam caught sight of Rosey creeping out of his light twenty or thirty metres away, slowly moving like some shy night creature.

Tam flicked off the beam and ran on.

'There's a bloody raid on!'

The man was gaining fast. Winnie had gone. But the darkness was on his side now. As the feet got near Tam suddenly slipped off the path and crawled into some tall plants – peas or beans – growing on one of the plots. The man was fooled. He ran past a couple of steps and paused.

'I know you're in there,' he yelled.

Tam waited, stayed still.

'Do you want to get yerself killed!' demanded the man. He began to move to and fro, peering this way and that through the darkness. Then he shouted – what he was really worried about, because he knew all too well that there would be no bombs on Cawldale that or any night: 'If I find any of my veg gone when I come back I'll have your blood. I'll have ARP on to you,' he added. Then he turned and made his way back the way he had come.

Tam waited a good five minutes. He wasn't going to blow his cover until he was really sure the man had gone. But before he got up he heard snuffling. Winnie reappeared, nose under his hand, shaking the plants with her tail as she crept in next to him.

'Have you got her?' whispered Tam. He crept out and followed the dog along the path. Winnie led him past one more plot to a little group of sheds. She turned the corner and then stood staring. She began to sniff. She glanced over her shoulder and whined. Tam understood. She had left May here, but now the old woman had gone again.

He dare not use his light, even though she might be only metres away. Winnie began circling again, seeking this way and that for the scent. This time Tam was determined not to let her run off. He grabbed hold of her collar and made her drag him. They went across the allotments, Winnie straining and gasping at her collar. Then across the cricket pitch to the edge of the streets. There were still a few people milling around. Tam held the collar firmly, although Winnie growled and pulled.

'We have to wait,' he said firmly. 'Sit ... sit!' She seemed to catch his urgency and sat down next to him, shuffling impatiently.

Ten minutes later they crept out from behind the fence and along the empty streets. Tam remembered how May had shown him how to go about at night. He paused at every street end, peered ahead and behind all the time. They saw no one. They crossed several streets, headed towards the town centre.

Then Tam knew where they were heading. It was somewhere he had been before. He understood that inside May did want him to find her after all. The tall houses disappeared and the back-to-backs began, tight little streets packed together, the moist, humid smell of people in poverty. In a few minutes they were at the edge of the little yard. Tam let go of Winnie's collar and she scrambled straight up the little hill of rubbish stacked against the wall.

Tam followed, found the skylight above the door. He didn't shine his torch for fear of scaring her. Then he heard her breath right beside him. She had not dared to drop down two metres now that she was old and weak.

He said, 'May,' uncertainly, heard the change in her breathing when she heard him. Tam reached out and with his hand under some boxes found her lying there. The dog lay across her. Tam pushed close and put his arm round her. She stiffened when he touched her but she didn't push him off.

'May,' he said.

The old woman's breath came faster and faster and she began to weep. For so long she had been still, for so long she had been without tears. She wanted to speak too, but she was unable to control her breath. When at last she found her voice, it was that strange, flat, fluting voice that Tam remembered from his days at Thowt It – creaking and honking now with age and lack of use – but it was May's voice.

She was saying, 'I got lost, Tam, I got lost for so long ...'

'But now I've found you,' he said.

Mrs Sams woke up suddenly. Pitch dark. Middle of the night. Someone was banging about downstairs. She glanced at the clock. Five o'clock! Five o'clock in the morning and someone was banging about in her house. She slid out of bed and into her slippers and gown and crept nervously along the landing to Tam's room. The bed was slept in but empty.

Her alarm began to turn to anger but she was still worried. Ever since he had disappeared that time she had been scared for him – scared of him, almost. She didn't understand her boy any more. She just prayed it wouldn't happen again.

She stamped downstairs. She could smell toast and that made her more annoyed. If he wanted to get up and have snacks at this time of night he could at least do it quietly – what a noise! Plates banging, doors slamming – she marched up the hall and flung open the kitchen door.

There was a dog in the middle of the floor eating pilchards in tomato sauce. She could see the tin on the table. It growled at her as she tried to get in and she had to hide behind the door. Tam had the entire contents of the fridge on the kitchen table and was dismembering last night's roast chicken with his hands. Worst of all, that hideous old bag lady that Mrs Caradine had brought home was sitting at the table drinking cocoa out of one of the best cups. In the neon light of the kitchen she looked positively disgusting. Her skin was black. To think that people lived like that in this day and age. And the pong! Someone must have dipped the old girl in the gutter.

Tam glared defiantly.

'Tam ...!' growled his mother. She was so taken aback she couldn't think.

The old woman tried to get up, but Tam stopped her. He did it gently as if she were a fragile china doll. 'She needs someone to help her,' he announced. His look challenged her to stop him.

'At five o'clock in the morning?' demanded his mother through gritted teeth.

'At any time!' snapped Tam. 'She's ...' He didn't

seem to find the words but he went suddenly up to the old woman and he put his arms around her and kissed her.

Mrs Sams's hand shot up to her mouth. Shocking, it was shocking to watch. That filthy, filthy mad old woman. 'He's mad,' she thought. She suddenly found herself hurrying across the floor to separate them – her clean boy kissing that wretched old thing. But the dog growled again and she stopped in her tracks.

The old woman raised her arm and put her dark old hand on Tam's, and she smiled up at him. It was a real smile – not the broken remains of one that she had seen on her face before, but a real, tender, affectionate smile. It was the first time she had seen any real expression on Rosey's face.

'I want her to live with us,' demanded Tam.

Mrs Sams licked her lips. She glanced back down the hall where the telephone sat on the table under the mirror. Should she? One call – the police? The Social Services? But she managed to smile grimly. 'And the dog, too?' she asked.

'She's mine... ours, I mean,' said Tam. 'She's called Winnie, after Winston Churchill.' The dog looked up from the pilchard sauce and wagged her tail.

Mrs Sams felt deeply out of depth. Tam was mad, the old woman was mad, she was mad for just standing there and not flinging her out. But look at the way the old woman was looking around her – alert, intelligent. It was as if the boy had brought her back from the dead.

Now, the filthy old creature was getting to her feet,

looking Mrs Sams straight in the eye like a normal human being. She began to speak – or at least to try to. Her mouth worked but what came out was a strange honking noise, like a strangulated goose. She was pointing at Tam and explaining something in confident tones and expressions as if it was all clear, simple English. Tam listened with his head on one side and smiled at her when she'd finished. He seemed to understand, he smiled and nodded as if all was perfectly clear and Mrs Sams was the odd one, the mad one. He made no attempt to explain it to her, though. The old woman pointed at her and said something but Tam just shook his head.

'It's no use,' he said. Rosey sat down and smiled and made a gesture at Mrs Sams as if to say, 'Sorry, I tried!' Tam got to buttering the toast. He watched his mother out of the corner of his eye to see what she would do next.

Mrs Sams glanced longingly at the telephone. She didn't want this, she didn't know how to deal with it.

'Well,' she said. 'After she's eaten, perhaps we could give Rosey a bath – what do you say, Rosey?'

Her son seemed wild. 'Her name's May,' he shouted. 'May, May!'

## READ MORE IN PUFFIN

For children of all ages, Puffin represents quality and variety – the very best in publishing today around the world.

For complete information about books available from Puffin – and Penguin – and how to order them, contact us at the appropriate address below. Please note that for copyright reasons the selection of books varies from country to country.

**On the worldwide web**: www.penguin.co.uk

**In the United Kingdom**: Please write to *Dept. EP, Penguin Books Ltd, Bath Road, Harmondsworth, West Drayton, Middlesex UB7 ODA*

**In the United States**: Please write to *Penguin Putnam inc., P.O. Box 12289, Dept B, Newark, New Jersey 07101-5289* or call 1-800-788-6262

**In Canada**: Please write to *Penguin Books Canada Ltd, 10 Alcorn Avenue, Suite 300, Toronto, Ontario M4V 3B2*

**In Australia**: Please write to *Penguin Books Australia Ltd, P.O. Box 257, Ringwood, Victoria 3134*

**In New Zealand**: Please write to *Penguin Books (NZ) Ltd, Private Bag 102902, North Shore Mail Centre, Auckland 10*

**In India**: Please write to *Penguin Books India Pvt Ltd, 11 Panscheel Shopping Centre, Panscheel Park, New Delhi 110 017*

**In the Netherlands**: Please write to *Penguin Books Netherlands bv, Postbus 3507, NL-1001 AH Amsterdam*

**In Germany**: Please write to *Penguin Books Deutschland GmbH, Metzlerstrasse 26, 60594 Frankfurt am Main*

**In Spain**: Please write to *Penguin Books S. A., Bravo Murillo 19, 1° B, 28015 Madrid*

**In Italy**: Please write to *Penguin Italia s.r.l., Via Felice Casati 20, I–20124 Milano*

**In France**: Please write to *Penguin France S. A., 17 rue Lejeune, F–31000 Toulouse*

**In Japan**: Please write to *Penguin Books Japan, Ishikiribashi Building, 2–5–4, Suido, Bunkyo-ku, Tokyo 112*

**In South Africa**: Please write to *Longman Penguin Southern Africa (Pty) Ltd, Private Bag X08, Bertsham 2013*

PUFFIN BOOKS

# An Angel for May

Melvin Burgess was born in 1954 and was brought up in Sussex and Berkshire. After leaving school he moved to Bristol, where he was generally unemployed, with occasional jobs, mainly in the building industry. He wrote, on and off, unsuccessfully. His first book, *The Cry of the Wolf*, was published in 1990.

Melvin Burgess writes full time and lives in Manchester with his wife and their children.

*Other books by Melvin Burgess*

THE EARTH GIANT

*For older readers*

THE BABY AND FLY PIE
THE CRY OF THE WOLF
KITE
LOVING APRIL
TIGER, TIGER